Derailed

In an unimaginable turn of events an outlaw gang had kidnapped the Colorado & Eastern train, leaving the passengers afoot in an early winter blizzard.

Tango and Ned Chambers are the men hired to prevent such things from happening. They are left alone on the frozen prairie with the wealthy and attractive widow Lady Simpson and a brother of the Vice-President of the United States as their charges.

Now all they have to do is recover the train, get through to Denver, and bring to justice those responsible for the outrage, without allowing harm to come to Lady Simpson and the politician.

Derailed

Owen G. Irons

A Black Horse Western

ROBERT HALE · LONDON

© Owen G. Irons 2011
First published in Great Britain 2012

ISBN 978-0-7090-9218-6

Robert Hale Limited
Clerkenwell House
Clerkenwell Green
London EC1R 0HT

www.halebooks.com

Typeset by
Derek Doyle & Associates, Shaw Heath
Printed and bound in Great Britain by
CPI Antony Rowe, Chippenham and Eastbourne

ONE

Ned Chambers passed the lanky blond-haired kid with his legs stretched out on the facing seat and made his way to the front of the railroad car. He recognized Tango, of course, and he knew that Drew Tango, hat pulled down over his eyes, had noted his passing. They were on the same side, but had different responsibilities. Tango and Chambers were both railroad security men. Tango was known for his gun skills and ability to spot the grifters on board at a glance. He was also just a little too quick to shoot and was rough around the edges in manner.

Ned Chambers was the smoother sort. He never wore a weapon that could be seen, was impeccably barbered and wore a neatly pressed dark suit. He was along to watch the special passengers headed for Colorado. Two of them were very special, indeed.

Lady Marina Simpson, an American girl who had gone to England and married a British aristo-crat, now deceased, was returning home. Besides a faint British accent, she was also carrying close to half a million dollars in jewelry. It was a secret, of course, but matters like that did not remain secret long. The New York newspapers had interviewed her on her arrival, and the reports of her fabulous collection had filtered West.

The other passenger Ned had been dispatched to keep a close eye on was Adam Wilson, the younger brother of the vice-president of the United States, Henry Wilson. His given reason for traveling to Colorado was a vacation. Many people thought there was more to it. Colorado was thriv-ing with new gold and silver strikes almost daily, and it was well known that neither President Grant nor his vice-president had ever so much as crossed to the western side of the Mississippi, and had no real knowledge of the far lands.

It was speculation, but seemed to be based on solid evidence, that the real purpose of Wilson's trip West was to test the political waters there con-cerning statehood – a proposition vigorously opposed by the mining interests in Colorado.

Ned Chambers had met both of the luminaries entrusted to his protection. Adam Wilson was a drinking man, heavy enough to be described as rotund, with a florid face and seemingly unkempt mustache the color of wheat straw. He was hardly prepossessing, but the balding little man seemed to have the energy of a dynamo flickering behind his pale, watery eyes.

Lady Marina Simpson, on the other hand was languid, drily humorous and startlingly attractive for a woman who already had strands of gray among the raven-black of her hair. She could easily have charmed a nobleman – she could have charmed a king. But she was not haughty and gave no indication that she had ever been a grasping or status-seeking woman. She spoke plainly but thoughtfully. She was not widely read, but her native intelligence was evident. She had told Ned Chambers that she had been born in a one-room log cabin, and when she moved up in the world she took the memory of the hard life on the plains with her, counting herself only lucky, not clever in the way she had arranged her life. Now she was returning home, not to wait for death but, as she put it, 'To see how gently one can age surrounded by the wild country.' She had not wanted to die penned up in a castle, and when her husband passed away, she had packed up and come back to the rugged land of her birth.

Ned Chambers found that he liked each of the two in different ways. Wilson was blunt in his opinions, but seemed to carefully consider any opposing view. True, he was in his sleeper room most of the day and night, drinking bourbon and playing cards with the small entourage accompanying him, but Chambers felt that he was focused on his mission – whatever that might be – and needed only to alight from the train to shift into action. That is, Wilson was only biding his time since nothing could be done at the moment, as the wood-burning locomotive clanked and huffed and plowed its way westward.

Lady Marina met Ned Chambers in the corridor in the next car. All of the sleepers had an aisle to one side of the train, accommodations on the other. Lady Marina stood at the windows lining the corridor, elbows on the brass sill. Glancing up, she smiled at Ned. Beyond the window twilight was settling, casting deep-purple light across the plains.

'I was hoping to catch sight of an Indian village,' she admitted. 'Funny, when I was a girl out here the very mention of an Indian sighting sent me into a panic, enough so that I would hide under my bed, shivering. Now I think I would give anything to see some wandering Cheyenne.'

'You'll see plenty of them not a few hours on,' Ned Chambers told her. 'Though not near the cities, of course. Is that where you're traveling to – Denver?'

'It was my plan, certainly. Now I wonder if I belong in Denver – in any city – though I don't know what I'd do with myself in the country now,' she added with a cheerful little laugh. 'It's unde-cided, I'd have to say. I've had enough of cities – Rome, London, New York, but how long would it take the lonely prairie nights to pale?' She looked wistful.

'I'm sure there's time to consider all of that, Lady Marina,' Ned answered. 'It's not a decision you have to make today, and you can always change your mind. Or, in your situation, you could proba-bly afford both a town house and a country place.'

'I'd never thought of that,' she said, straighten-ing to look up at him. 'But when you mention my situation, I have to believe you are probably labor-ing under a misapprehension. Death taxes, bequeathals to other family members by my late husband, have left me with little more than I have on my back, or around my neck.' She touched the diamond necklace at her throat with her long, tapered fingers which also sported diamonds.

'These jewels are not evidence of my vast wealth – they are my only wealth, Mr Chambers. If I were to lose them. . . .'

'That's why I am here, Lady Marina,' Ned Chambers replied, trying for a confident smile. 'You needn't worry about train robbers.'

What a liar I am, Ned thought as he continued toward the back of the train. As soon as the first tracks had been laid for the railroad, outlaws had focused on the opportunity. Now, instead of having to ride to where the money was, the railroad was delivering it to them, and there was no pursuit after a train robbery. The thieves simply disappeared on the plains while the passengers could do nothing but stare after them. Train robberies were increasing every year in all parts of the country, but especially out here, where the nearest law might be a hundred miles away and unable or unwilling to track down the hold-up men.

Which was where men like Ned and Drew Tango came in. True, their jobs were different: Tango's specialty was trading lead with men trying to rob the train or otherwise stir up a ruckus. Ned Chambers was a sort of detective, if you will, whose job was to discover trouble in the making and prevent it, especially when it came to dignitaries.

Ned saw Lady Marina to her compartment, cautioned her again to keep the door locked, and had started back up the aisle when he was nearly jerked from his feet by the engineer applying the brakes – hard.

Out here on the open plains with nothing but flat ground to travel across, the sudden application could mean only one thing to Ned Chambers: they had trouble, and serious trouble. He drew his Russian .36 revolver from where it rode in a holster at the back of his belt and hurried forward.

Drew Tango had been lounging in his seat when the brakes were applied. Without hesitation, Tango leapt to his feet and pushed through the front door of railroad car, to be met by freezing cold and the acrid smells of oil and burning wood.

He mounted the tender, crossed the piles of fuel wood there and descended toughly on to the steel-plate deck of the locomotive cab.

'What's happening?' he asked the engineer, Frank Polk, who was leaning out of the cab, looking down the tracks. His fireman, Danny Short, was at his elbow.

'Have a look,' Frank growled and Drew Tango leaned far out. A steam valve hissed and released a cloud of white vapour, blurring his vision temporarily. When it cleared Tango could see the

11

reason for Polk's caution. Someone had built a bonfire square in the middle of the tracks, a mile or so ahead. It blazed brightly, though at this distance it was not much larger than a firefly's light.

'What do you think, Tango?' Polk asked in a worried voice.

'It looks like a robbery for sure,' Drew had to say as he turned to face the engineer in the glow of the firebox.

'What should I do – try to run through it?'

'You can't know if they've torn up the rails on the other side of it,' Tango replied. 'If you try to run it, they'll be sure to open up with their weapons. We don't want a lot of passengers shot up.'

Tango glanced at the purpling skies. The robbers had chosen the right time of day for their ambush. They would be uncertain shadows in the darkness, and an attempt of this sort was never made without a large body of men.

'Aren't we going to fight them?' Danny Short, young and wild-eyed, demanded.

'I don't see how,' Tango answered honestly.

'Well, damnit!' the young fireman shouted. 'Isn't that what you're here for? Where's Mr Chambers?'

'He's busy right now. Look, Frank,' Tango said

to the engineer, 'give it a few minutes and then start forward again – keep your speed down—'

'And hope for the best!' Danny Short squeaked nervously.

'And hope for the best,' Drew Tango said. He briefly placed a hand on the engineer's shoulder and again clambered up on to the wood-tender. As he dropped down to the platform below he found Ned Chambers waiting for him, pistol in hand.

'What's up?' Chambers asked.

'It's a hold-up. We've got about five minutes to get Lady Simpson and Wilson off the train.'

'You think it's one of them they're after?'

'Don't you?' Tango answered. 'If it's just a gang of bandits who want to walk through the aisles, collecting wallets and rings, well, the railroad can apologize and shrug it off as just one of the hazards of traveling in rough country; apologize and be forgiven. If we lose Lady Simpson and her jewels or the vice-president's brother, we've got more than an incident, we've got hell to pay.'

'All right,' Ned said without enthusiasm. 'I suppose you're right, Tango. Let's get those people off the train.'

Eyes lifted as Tango and Ned hurried back through the passenger cars toward the sleeper, but no one demanded to know what was happening.

Lady Simpson was awake and alert when they found her at the door to her room. 'We've got to get off the train,' Ned Chambers told her. 'Grab a change of clothes and secure your jewelry.'

'Yes, I'll be right with you,' she said without question. That was one well-fashioned lady, Ned decided. No screaming, no tears, just action.

The same could not be said for Adam Wilson. Tango had already knocked on the door of the vice-president's brother and it had been opened to exude the rough smells of whiskey and tobacco fumes. There was another man visiting Wilson, and as Ned approached he could hear both of them arguing with Tango.

'What are you talking about?' the slender, sallow visitor was objecting. 'Why should we get off here?'

'For your safety,' Tango tried and Ned could tell that the hot-blooded Drew Tango was making an extreme effort to restrain himself. Ned took over, arming Tango out of the way.

'We have reason to believe, Mr Wilson, that there are bandits up ahead who may be there for the purpose of capturing you.'

'Those robber-baron profiteers! The big mine-owners?'

'That's possible,' Ned answered calmly. 'We can't really be sure. We only feel that for your personal safety it is urgent that you exit the train. Within the next few minutes. The train will be moving forward again shortly.'

'I have no fear of robbers and brigands,' Wilson said, striking a political pose. 'If they think they or anyone can thwart the will of the people of Colorado to achieve statehood by using such tactics—'

'Let's get going, Mr Wilson!' Tango snapped. 'Grab a coat and any important documents you have and let's get moving.'

'And who are you, young man?' the pale, sharp-faced man who was with Wilson demanded arrogantly.

'The man who's going to save your hide if you listen to me,' Drew Tango said as they felt the train lurch beneath their feet. 'We have to go *now*!'

'This is unconscionable,' the man said, skittering on his boots as the train jerked again. 'I am Senator Ruben Knox of Delaware.'

'I don't care if you're the King of Prussia, we've got to get going.'

'I demand personal security!' Knox sputtered.

'You'll have to go back to Delaware for that,' Tango said. 'Right now I want you to go to the rear platform and exit this train.'

Wilson seemed to have understood the peril by

now. He wore a winter coat into which he tucked a bundle of official-looking letters. Senator Knox had taken a belligerent posture, arms crossed defiantly. Wilson took Knox by the shoulders and said, 'Ruben, we have to take these men at their word. They are in charge of security matters out here.'

Knox appeared ready to argue further, but surrendered his obstinacy at Wilson's request and followed them out into the corridor, where Lady Simpson was waiting for them, holding a small leather satchel.

'What's this?' Wilson wanted to know. 'What's she got to do with this?'

'That's just it,' Ned Chambers told him. 'We don't know.'

When they reached the rear platform the train was still only going a few miles an hour as the great drive-wheels on the 4-4-2 locomotive fought for purchase against the iron rails. It was bitterly cold, and smoke and embers drifted along the spine of the train and flowed over them. Tango nodded to Chambers and swung over to the ladder. He dropped from the train and hit the ground running, but at that speed it wasn't much of a trick to stay upright. He called up to Lady Marina.

'Toss me your bag, then get to the bottom step.

I'll catch you as you jump!'

Without hesitation Lady Marina Simpson tossed her bag to Tango, who was now trotting alongside the train. Then, astonishing all of them, she went down to the lowest step and leaped quite nimbly to the ground, holding her skirts high.

'There's more to you than a person would think.' Tango laughed as he handed her valise back.

'I'm still spry enough for an occasional game,' she answered, panting.

Adam Wilson was a different story. The pudgy man hesitated too long, and the train continued to pick up speed. Watching the dark, rock-strewn land rush past he was frozen with indecision. Ned Chambers continued to encourage the man, gently at first and then more harshly.

'If you don't jump now, you won't be able to,' Ned shouted above the rush of the wind. 'And those people up ahead are after your blood.'

His eyes wide with panic, Wilson bleated an unintelligible word, looked into Ned's eyes for pity and finally stepped off into space, hitting the ground hard enough to make keeping his feet impossible. He rolled down the embankment roughly as Lady Simpson and Tango rushed to aid him. Ned Chambers wasted no time on the other man, Senator Knox. He shouldered the man roughly, practically throwing him from the train. Ned followed, taking three running steps as he hit the ground before his feet went out from under him and he fell, skinning his knees and the heels of his hands.

Tango was striding toward him, grinning. 'Took your time about it,' Drew Tango said.

'Where's the train?' Ned growled, standing to dust himself off in the purple night.

'It looks like Frank is braking to a stop just this side of the bonfire.'

The two railroad operatives stood together, watching events as Wilson, Knox and Lady Simpson caught up with them. Two shots rang out near the train and Ned saw Wilson flinch.

'Who are they shooting?' he asked nervously, peering along the track toward halted train.

'I'd guess those were just to warn people that they were serious,' Tango answered.

'What are they doing now?' Marina Simpson asked. She was clinging to Ned Chambers's arm, shivering as night settled in. A few drops of rain hit Tango's face as he stared at the halted train.

'They're unloading the passengers,' he said.

'Why?' Knox asked irritably.

'Searching for something, I'd think.'

'For Adam Wilson?'

'I won't try to outguess them,' Tango said. The rain, which had begun with a few scattered drops, now began to hammer briskly down, a cold wind driving it. The gloom of the evening was almost complete, though some diffused purple light showed among the black clouds.

'We've got to do something,' Adam Wilson said. 'The temperature's dropped at least ten degrees since we've been standing here. If we don't find shelter we'll freeze to death.'

'Thanks to these two,' Ruben Knox said bitterly. 'We could be in our compartment, safe and warm.'

'You could also be the two men those shots were meant for,' Ned Chambers said roughly.

'Look!' Marina Simpson said excitedly, pointing along the tracks. 'The train is moving again.'

It was, and by the luminescent flare of lightning, they could see that it had left without its passengers. These stood in a straggling line along the rails. A couple of men ran after the train briefly before giving it up as the locomotive again gathered speed.

'We have to get up there with the others,' Wilson insisted.

'We can't know if the train robbers left a guard behind,' Tango cautioned. 'Beides I can't see that

19

it would do us or them any good to join the others.'

'Then what do you suggest!' Ruben Knox demanded.

It was a good question. The rain swept over them and the wind grew colder as the storm swept in from the east, off the high Rockies. They were isolated, unsheltered and abandoned in the darkness of a Colorado winter storm. The lights of the train, their last hope of contact with civilization, swept around a bend and were extinguished by the darkness. There was only the faint scent of woodsmoke hanging in the air to remind them that it had ever been there.

TWO

They trudged northward, away from the railroad tracks into the darkness as the rain slanted down and the skies grumbled. The going was over rough night-shrouded ground, and each of them had slipped more than once and fallen heavily. Ned Chambers kept his grip on Lady Simpson's arm. Wilson and Ruben Knox trudged on without even the strength to snap and curse at Tango, who was leading them on into the wilderness.

'I know where we are,' Tango had told Ned Chambers as they had cast about for a plan of action. 'Do you know Cinnamon Bluffs?'

'Only by mention. I can't remember anything I've heard about it.'

'I caught sight of it through a break in the storm,' Tango told them. 'There used to be a stage stop there – before the railroad came through and made it irrelevant. It's been deserted for more than two years.'

'Then of what use is it to us?' the contrary Knox wanted to know.

'Plenty,' Tango said, 'if it still has a roof on it. We can shelter up there out of the wind and rain until we can come up with a better plan. It beats standing alongside the tracks in this weather waiting for the next train to come, which seems to be what all of the other passengers are doing.'

'I'd like to vote for joining the other passengers,' Wilson said. Ned Chambers was sharp in his response.

'This isn't a democracy, sir.' Then to Tango: 'Let's get going if you know the way, Drew. We could all freeze to death standing here, debating.'

So they trudged northward, the gusting wind driving rain against their cheeks and eyes, the temperature dropping precipitously. Even Tango began to have doubts as he trudged on across the wasteland, at times slogging through mud and pools of icy water. He did know where he was going, but by daylight, along a marked road, the shuttered stage station was much easier to locate than trying to find it in these conditions.

The lash and whip of the wind drove icy rain

against their faces; the constant growl of thunder threatened more of the same weather, and the way the temperature kept dropping indicated that the rain would soon turn to snow. Then what? Wandering around the plains in a smothering snow storm would very likely prove fatal. Tango felt the fool at that moment; he was glad he could not hear the words being considered behind the glaring, suffering eyes of Adam Wilson and Ruben Knox.

'I see something, Tango,' Ned Chambers called above the torrent of rain. All eyes looked hopefully in the direction Ned indicated, but no one saw a thing. Then lightning flared again, close at hand and Tango, too, saw the dumpy form of the deserted way station.

'Let's get moving before we lose it again,' Tango said. Thunder followed on the heels of his command, shaking the earth underfoot.

It was a half-hour farther on when, exhausted and soaked to the skin, they came upon the pole and adobe structure that had been a way station for the coach line before this section of it had been discontinued, the line running farther south now, through Winston and Adobe Wells where there was no competition from the railroad.

Ned pushed at the warped, weather-beaten door

and it gave, allowing them entrance. It was unusually warm inside, or at least it seemed to be. There was the feel in the air of fire not long extinguished.

Beyond the window now they could see the snow starting to fall. A few thick flakes pasted themselves against the glass pane, and the strengthening wind shook the small structure. Ruben Knox stood shivering in his rain-saturated coat, arms wrapped tightly around him. He was not alone when he suggested, 'We should start a fire before we freeze to death.' They all agreed.

'You don't think that smoke would give us away?' Tango asked Ned Chambers.

'We don't even know if anyone's looking for us. Besides, that wind will whip the smoke away. I think it's safe enough.'

'All right,' Tango answered, 'if we can find any wood.'

Lady Simpson, who had gone exploring, told them, 'There's a bin filled with coal in the kitchen.'

'That'll do the job,' Ned replied. 'You others, shovel out the fireplace. I saw a bucket out front you can dump the residue in.'

'I guess that means me,' Tango said, looking at Knox and Wilson, neither of whom apparently wished to dirty his hands. Catching Tango's look,

Knox protested hurriedly.

'I am, after all, the senator from Delaware.'

'That might mean something somewhere,' Tango snapped. 'Me, I don't even know where Delaware is and if folks back there are like you, I don't intend to ever go there.'

'Meaning?' Knox said huffily.

'Meaning if a man is freezing to death and too lazy to build a fire to warm up by, he deserves to freeze.'

'That's enough, Tango,' Ned Chambers said before things could get out of hand. Tango clamped his jaw shut. Ned was not technically his boss, but Tango respected the older man and knew that he himself had a habit of going off, taking things too personally. He stepped out into the wash and swirl of the settling storm, looked for the bucket, found it and entered the room again.

'Does it look like a big storm?' Adam Wilson asked.

'Big enough,' Tango answered, crouching by the fireplace. 'We're not going anywhere anytime soon.'

'I knew it was a big mistake to leave the train,' Senator Knox complained.

'Sure,' Tango said, shoveling the ash from the grate. 'We could all now be standing comfortably

25

beside the tracks in the middle of a blizzard. No wonder they elected you.'

Tango worked silently, filling the bucket and emptying it outside twice before Ned came carrying coal from the kitchen bin. Lady Simpson had gone reconnoitering again. This time when she returned she was wearing twill trousers, a light suede jacket over a white blouse and had her long dark hair tied back in a pony tail.

'You adapt quickly,' Ned said to her.

'One of my more endearing qualities,' Marina Simpson laughed. 'Really, when you find yourself where you are – there you are – may as well make the best of it.' She finished arranging her hair as she spoke. 'Did I hear someone say we're not traveling on tonight?'

'Or tomorrow, at a guess,' Ned said.

'Just as well. For myself I'm hungry and tired. There are beds in four back rooms, and a scattering of food in the kitchen. I found a sack of potatoes which belong in the ground and not on the table, but we'll give them a trim and a shave and some of them are probably salvageable. Who's a hand with a paring knife?'

'I suppose that will have to be me,' Tango said sourly.

'I'll do it, Tango,' Ned interjected. 'Dry yourself

and see to the fire.'

Tango glanced at Ned questioningly. Ned wasn't exactly what they called smitten with Lady Simpson, but he was definitely interested in her. He lifted a hand in agreement and watched the two walk across the dusty floor toward the kitchen.

'We'd better have a look at those bedrooms,' Adam Wilson said, 'if we're spending the night here.' He had found the stubs of two candles; he lit the wick of one from the fire in the hearth and started down the corridor.

'I just need a clean blanket,' Knox said as if he were now roughing it.

'Good luck,' Tango couldn't help saying. 'There hasn't been anyone staying here for two years. If you find any blanket at all, count yourself lucky.'

But Tango wondered as he watched the two city men wander down the dark hallway if he were speaking the truth. Yes, the place was dusty, the furniture rotting away, but he felt that someone had been using the stage station. Maybe groups of travelers on their way to or from Denver and Leadville, but someone, he felt, had been there quite recently. For one thing there was the relative warmth of the house when they had first entered it. And the embers from the fireplace had not been cool yet, as he had discovered painfully.

There had been a cigar end among the refuse and, fingering it, Tango had found that it was not brittle and dry. Someone was around, or had been, not long before. Unbuttoning his coat, Tango seated himself in one of the torn leather chairs near the door, his Colt ready to hand. In the kitchen he could hear Ned and Lady Simpson, who had become simply Marina, talking in low tones. Tango pulled the bottle of whiskey he had paused long enough to pilfer from the railroad's stores from his coat pocket and opened it. It was fiery, warming and the coal fire was burning nicely behind the grate.

Why then did Tango feel an icy chill crawling up his spine?

When Ned Chambers returned from the kitchen a few minutes later he was wearing an apron wrapped around his hips. He told Tango:

'Way in the back of the larder I found two tins of corned beef. Of course there wasn't much of those potatoes by the time we cut out the bad spots, but there's enough for a rough kind of hash.' He was smiling with satisfaction. Tango did not return the smile.

'We've got company,' he told Ned, nodding toward the door.

'Are you sure?'

'I heard them. A horse doesn't make much noise walking across snow, with the wind whipping around, but I'm sure.'

'How many?' Ned asked with concern.

'I can't be sure, but more than one certainly.'

'I'd better talk to the others,' Ned said, casting another uneasy glance at the door.

'You'd better,' Tango agreed. 'Tell them to get this right.'

Ned thought he heard a boot stepping up on to the porch and he nodded. 'Tango, if they come in, why don't you sit away from the rest of us and just keep an eye on things.'

'That's what I was intending to do,' Tango said. He seated himself again in the tattered leather chair, shifting his holster more comfortably. Across the room he could see Ned speaking rapidly to the other three.

'I'll do most of the talking,' Ned was saying. 'Just take your cues from me and add as little as possible.'

'All right,' Adam Wilson agreed. He looked worried but not deeply frightened. Knox was another proposition. The thin, sharp-faced senator had panic in his eyes.

'What if they. . . ?'

Then everyone fell silent as the front door,

29

assisted by the gusting wind blew open and slammed against the wall of the way station. They saw four men standing there. These eyed the gathering for a long minute, then entered. The first man in, presumably their leader, was tall and wide-shouldered, wore a snow-dusted sheepskin coat and a Stetson pulled down low. He was followed by two more rough-looking characters and, trailing them, a slender kid of nineteen or so who had two crossed front teeth and a sort of subdued madness behind his blue eyes. Tango thought this was the one to keep his eyes on.

The big man stepped forward to meet Ned Chambers who had taken charge of matters. 'I'm Chris Stilton,' he said extending a thick, weather-cut hand.

'John Hilton,' Ned replied, taking his rough hand.

'These two are brothers, Nathan and Freeman Cole,' said Stilton, introducing the two men standing beside him. They were of a type, long curly black hair, hawkish noses and silent dark eyes. 'And that back there is Mickey Dent. Close the damn door, Mickey!'

The kid's eyes filled with a poisonous glare which seemed to be aimed at no one in particular, and he went to the door, slamming it shut against the whip of the wind and the steadily falling snow.

'This is Mr Hollis Crater,' Ned said, nodding at Adam Wilson. 'Owner of the Double Tree ranch down in Socorro. That's his brother, Hugh.'

'Howdy,' Stilton said with a nod. 'And the lady?'

'That's my daughter, Beth,' Adam Wilson said, catching on to the game.

Stilton nodded at Marina and glanced toward the kitchen. 'Something smells good; do you mind if we join you?'

'We have very little,' said Marina. She had exchanged her British accent for the Western drawl of her youth, 'But you boys are welcome to share what we have.'

'Up all the way from Socorro, huh?' Stilton said, rocking on his heels in front of the low-burning coal fire.

'The way those Denver and Leadville mines are going,' Ned improvised, 'they're going to need beef for the miners. We mean to provide it if Mr Crater can come to terms with the mine bosses. The train West was held up, and we took shelter here.'

'Which mines are you talking about?' Stilton inquired. It could have been a trick. Ned looked to Wilson, who took over easily. 'It's a consortium of five different mine owners – I'm not sure I can recall the names of any of the mines right now. Nor is it of any importance to me.'

'I see,' Stilton answered. He had been eye-balling the group as he warmed himself at the fire. None of them looked like ranchers to him, but then even everyday cowboys did their best to clean up and put on fancy duds when heading for town. He supposed the owner of a big ranch had no use for a range outfit. There was Tango. That one looked ready to spend a day roping and branding or droving cattle. 'Who's that?' Stilton asked, nodding at Tango.

'Sonny?' Ned asked, glancing that way. He had to limit the conversation. He was afraid he would forget the names he had given to everyone. 'He'll be our trail boss. He wanted to get a look at the country he'd be pushing the cattle over.'

Tango only nodded. He didn't want to get roped into the game for the same reason as Ned. Even now he had forgotten the senator's new name, and he was afraid of blurting something out. He sat back again, reaching for the bottle of whiskey beside him. Mickey Dent saw the bottle and his eyes lit up.

'I'll have me some of that,' he said eagerly, and he reached for the whiskey. Tango glared at the kid. He did nothing to prevent Dent from taking

32

the bottle, though the idea had crossed his mind.

'Mickey,' Stilton scolded as the kid drank three or four fingers of whiskey from the bottle, 'Haven't I been teaching you to ask before reaching?'

Tango decided then and there that he didn't like Mickey and he didn't like Chris Stilton. Stilton's eyes had shown amusement. Perhaps he had decided now that Tango posed no threat to them.

They all sat to the table – except Tango – and Ned and Marina brought in the serving of hash, which divided into half, seemed barely adequate. Stilton talked as he ate, directing most of his words toward Adam Wilson.

'Well, Mr Crater, the reason I was asking about which mines you had it in mind to deliver your beef to is that we work for the mine operators – or will when we can get there. We have jobs as regulators out there.'

'Regulators?' Wilson asked as if the term were new to him, and perhaps it was.

'We provide security for the mines,' Stilton said around a mouthful of hash. 'Keep the bad element away from the goldfields.'

Which meant, Ned knew, that they were simply hired thugs. Their job was to keep any independent prospectors out of the rich areas, to retaliate if miners were caught sampling the mines' ores and, more important to the mine bosses, to crush any attempt by the miners to organize the workers in that brutal high country where twelve hours a day was spent underground, twelve in flimsy tents with the cold of winter settling in.

Men who fought against conditions frequently had to be 'regulated.'

'What'd you say happened to that train you were on?' Stilton asked.

'We don't know exactly. It was stopped on the tracks and we started hearing gunfire,' Ned answered. 'It seemed prudent to leave.'

'I guess you must be carrying valuables?' Stilton asked slyly.

'No, you can't keep cattle in a purse,' Wilson replied with just the right touch. Stilton actually smiled, but it was not reassuring. Everyone in the cabin now was aware that they had fallen among thieves and toughs.

The brothers, Nathan and Freeman Cole, had long ago finished their meager meal and sat stiffly in their chairs. Mickey Dent had finished eating as well, but the kid jittered nervously in his seat as if incapable of sitting still. He leaped abruptly to his feet.

'I believe I'll have some more whiskey. Anyone

want to join me?'

'Remember to ask the man,' Stilton admonished sardonically.

'Sure!' Dent laughed, striding across the room to where Tango sat, expressionless. 'Mind if I take some more whiskey, friend?' he asked.

'Go ahead,' Tango answered.

'See, Mickey,' Stilton said, 'being polite has its benefits.'

'It can keep you from getting shot, for one thing,' Tango said, and he was not kidding. Ned knew that, and everyone else in the room caught the menace in Tango's voice. Ned shook his head slightly at Tango. This was no time to go off half-cocked. Not now. Not here in an enclosed space with innocent people – including Marina – around. Mickey Dent gave Tango a startled look which changed into a sarcastic grin. He grabbed the bottle by the neck and returned to the table, figuring he and his companions had backed Tango down.

Walking into the kitchen where Marina and Ned Chambers were cleaning up as the other men shared Tango's bottle of whiskey at the table, Tango asked, 'Have you got the sleeping arrangements all worked out?' Beyond the small four-paned window he could see nothing of the land through the dark screen of the snowstorm. Ned frowned, wiping his hands on a torn towel.

'I think so. Marina in her own room at the back, Wilson, Knox and myself in the room adjacent, our four guests in the two rooms opposite. You, I suppose. . . .'

'I'll be spending the night in that chair. I advise you to keep your gun close to hand.'

'I intended to; why the advice?'

'We may not be as tricky as we think we are, or maybe they're a little smarter. They've got Wilson and Senator Knox drinking with them now. Whiskey's not known to sharpen the mind. A few seemingly offhand questions would be enough to reveal that Wilson is no cattleman.

'It could also be that there's no need to resort to trickery. They could have been a part of the hold-up, you know. Why should we take Stilton's word about them being regulators? They could already know who Wilson is; they could be part of a plan to assassinate him.'

'You're right, of course,' Ned said furrowing his brow, placing the dishrag aside. 'I haven't been thinking as clearly as you.'

No, and there was a reason for that – the tall woman with the long dark hair. Women also were not known for sharpening a man's mind when he was swept up by one.

Ned said, 'I'd better try to get our charges bedded down.'

'I've seen Knox at his drinking,' Tango said. 'He won't want to go to bed until the last dog is hung.'

'I suppose not,' Ned replied, 'and I can't force him – keep your powder dry,' he said with a smile, briefly placing his hand on Tango's shoulder.

'I intend to. Tell me, are there locks on those doors?'

'No. Only hooks.'

'Then,' Tango said seriously, glancing at Marina who was busy putting dishes away as if this were her home, 'I'd recommend you keep your door open, Ned. We don't know who these men are, what they intend.'

As Tango returned to his chair in the living room, Marina asked Ned, 'What was that about? I only heard something about leaving our doors open.'

'Not you,' Ned answered. Feeling awkward, as if he were invading Marina's privacy, he placed both hands on her shoulders and told her. 'Tango thinks that something is up, that Stilton's men may try to do some prowling tonight. He has good instinct for that sort of thing – you might say it's a part of his job.'

'Oh,' Marina said, turning her eyes down, but not moving away from Ned Chambers, 'do you think they may know about my jewels?'

'We don't know what they may know, and that's just it,' Ned told her quietly, glancing toward the open door, where someone – Freeman Cole, possibly – erupted with loud laughter.

'I see,' Marina said, and now with a little shrug she did move away from Ned and go to the window where, with her arms crossed, she looked out at the rampaging storm. 'I don't know what it is, but I'm starting to feel a little cold. I believe I'll go to bed.'

'I'll be right next door, and wide awake.'

That was true. Weary as Ned was, he could not risk falling asleep with these men in the house. He felt that Tango was right. Someone meant to do evil in the way station on this night.

THREE

The coal fire was burning low. A soft reddish glow painted the walls and ceiling of the way station. Tango was relaxed and warm, comfortable in the torn leather chair, but he was not sleepy. Rather, he would not let himself grow sleepy. Despite the whiskey he had drunk earlier and the long tiring walk to reach this place he could not allow his body to lose its fighting edge. There would be trouble; he was sure of that.

Earlier, in the back of the house, he had heard Chris Stilton and his cronies loudly getting ready for bed, joking and grumbling, the high-pitched complaints of Mickey Dent sounding quite clearly. That, Tango did not care about. In his experience men who were up to no good were seldom noisy, boisterous. They prepared silently for their stealthy movements.

It was much later, when the house grew silent and the fire lost its glow as the storm rampaged on beyond the walls, that each small sound roused his curiosity. He waited, shivering now in the near-warmth of the room, listening to every sound audible above the roar and whistle of the wind.

Tango thought he heard movement and he rose to his feet. Someone getting out of bed? Drawing boots on silently? There was no telling. He eased toward the entrance to the hallway, drawing his gun, alert for any telltale sound, his eyes searching the dark extent of the corridor. There was the definite creak of a long unoiled door opening. Which of them he could not be sure. Except that it was not Ned Chambers's door. Ned would have taken Tango's advice and left his own door ajar. Tango, who was used to facing armed men in his work for the Colorado & Eastern, felt his heart rate begin to lift.

The door opened a little farther and Tango saw a shadowy figure creep out into the hall. And cross to Lady Simpson's door. He saw the man carefully try the door handle. Tango was going to have to call him down, no matter what happened. He only hoped that no one would recklessly dash out of the other rooms. Good as Tango was with a gun, he would be shooting half-blind and there would be no room for error if someone – Marina – got caught in a cross-fire. Tango felt that he could wait no longer as the intruder put his shoulder against Lady Simpson's door and began applying pressure.

'Stand away,' Tango ordered in a quiet voice. 'I've got you in my sights.'

'The hell with you,' the man, whose voice Tango now recognized to be that of Chris Stilton, snarled. Then he shouted, 'Come on, boys! We've got a man says he wants to shoot me.' There was a snorting laugh of bold confidence as Stilton spoke these last words and reached for his holstered pistol. Two men, the Cole brothers judging by their stature, emerged from the room. Tango fired first and saw one of the brothers spin around in a crazy sort of dance toward death. Before Tango could fire again, his brother had gone to a knee and sent a shot from that position in Tango's direction. Shooting back wildly, Tango rolled toward the shelter of the wall.

As he reached safety Tango heard the sharp crack of another, smaller-caliber revolver. Ned Chambers and his .36 caliber Remington had joined in the fight. Peering around the corner, Tango saw the other Cole brother standing against the wall, holding his chest. Moments later he slid down the wall into a seated position, his gun dropping free. Chris Stilton had not moved. Instead of firing his weapon he began cursing loudly, profanely.

'Give it up, Stilton,' Tango called. 'It's all over!'

'I guess it is,' Stilton answered and for a moment Tango thought the man was going to drop his weapon. Then what Tango had feared happened. A stubby figure burst into the corridor, waving angry hands.

'What's all this about!' Senator Ruben Knox demanded imperiously, and Stilton shot him. Tango took a duelist's position and fired twice at Stilton who dropped to the floor beside his victim.

'Tango?' Ned Chambers called from his room.

'It's all right. Come on out. Watch it though, there's still one of them barricaded in his room. Dent.'

Ned eased from his room, gun held high beside his ear. Adam Wilson saw the dead men, including his friend Knox. He staggered forward, moaning. 'I tried to stop him! Ruben always was so impetuous.'

Tango moved cautiously down the hallway to join Ned. He noticed that Lady Simpson had not opened her door. It seemed that she was good at taking orders. Marina was a good soldier.

Ned was at the outlaw's door. Tango moved up to the opposite side, nodded a signal and kicked the door open. A cold blast of winter air met them, blasting through a narrow, broken window. Ned Chandler eased to the window and looked out. He could easily make out Mickey Dent's bootprints, lining out toward the south, in the direction of the railroad tracks. Adam Wilson had come into the room behind them.

'The little coward bolted, did he?' Wilson asked.

'Could be,' Ned said, glancing at Tango. Wilson was puzzled. Ned explained it to him:

'It could be he just panicked and ran off, or it could be that he's on his way to get help. We don't know if these four were alone or if they were part of a larger gang: the ones who ambushed the train.'

'No, I suppose not,' Wilson said, thoughtfully nibbling at his lower lip. 'What are we to do then?'

'Get the hell out of here,' Tango said with emphasis. 'We've got four horses left by Stilton and his men.'

'And hundreds of miles to go,' Wilson said miserably.

'That's right,' Tango replied. They were aware now of Marina standing in the doorway behind them, her face pale after passing the carnage in the corridor.

'Is it over now?' she asked shakily, looking at them in turn. 'Ned? Tango?'

It was Ned Chambers who answered her. 'We can hope so, Marina, but I have the feeling that this was only the beginning of our troubles.'

She nodded. 'I'll get dressed. I heard Tango say we're going for a ride.'

'That's quite a woman,' Tango said after she was gone.

'You're just now noticing that?' Ned Chambers responded. Then he stalked off to get dressed, Wilson in his wake.

'I'm going to see what they left us in the way of horseflesh,' Tango called into Ned's room.

'All right,' Ned Chambers answered, emerging as he finished tucking in his shirt. 'I'll be getting these men out of here. They'd be a nasty surprise for the next traveler stopping by.'

'What are you going to do with them?' they heard Adam Wilson ask.

'All we can do – drag them around back. I hate to leave them to the critters, but there's nothing else to be done. We obviously can't dig graves out there just now. Even if we could, we don't want to be wasting the time to do it. Who knows if that Mickey Dent is going to come back with more riders.'

44

Wilson sighed heavily, nodding his head in agreement. 'You're right, of course, I'll give you a hand. Let me first remove any personal items from poor Ruben's pockets.'

Tango turned to leave, glad that for once he had not gotten the dirty job. He preferred live horses to dead men any time. His relief collapsed briefly as he opened the door and met the full force of the storm once more. The wind had not abated, and though the snowfall had lightened somewhat, the wind drove it into his face like thrown pebbles. Tango ducked his head and started on toward the stable.

There was not much left of the old place. Shingles had blown away, leaving gaping holes in the roof. There were gaps in the side walls as well, and the cold wind whipped through the building. Four horses lifted their heads from their stalls to warily watch Tango's approach. Tango walked to the first stall and lifted his hand to stroke the muzzle of a stolid looking buckskin horse.

'That's right, old-timer,' he said to the horse. 'I haven't got food for you, and I'm going to have to take you out in the weather again.'

Besides the buckskin there were two nearly identical roan horses – belonging to the Cole brothers? Also there was a smaller, younger paint pony with suspicious eyes. Maybe it had been Mickey Dent's mount. Tango got to work outfitting the ponies. By the time he was finished and had led the horses to the front of the house, tying them to the hitch rail where the storm flared their manes and tails, Ned Chambers and Wilson had finished their grisly work.

Marina stood in front of the hearth which contained only a memory of warmth. 'Are we ready to ride, Mr Tango?' she asked.

'I'm not,' he said with a brief laugh, 'but it looks like that's what we're going to do.'

Ned and Wilson emerged from the back room again, Wilson looking pale and weary. 'Are we set?' Ned Chambers asked.

'I brought the horses around.'

'How's the weather?' Wilson asked anxiously.

'Not good. The snow's letting up a little, it seems.'

'Well,' Wilson said dubiously. 'There's no choice, is there? Let's be moving.'

'Marina,' said Tango, who had dropped all of that 'Lady Simpson' stuff by now, 'one of the horses – a little paint pony, is more suitable for someone lighter. That will be your horse.'

'All right,' she said agreeably. Under her arm she held the leather satchel containing her jewelry. 'Are there saddle-bags?'

'They all had them with their saddles,' Tango assured her.

'Did you find anything inside the pouches?' Ned asked.

'I didn't take the time to look,' Tango told him. 'All of the horses were carrying rifles in their scabbards as well, though; they might be of some help.'

Ned just nodded. He hoped they would not run into another shooting situation, but had no confidence that this would prove so. Adam Wilson stood waiting miserably. 'I haven't had much experience riding,' he said.

'Just keep the horse loose-reined,' Ned advised. 'Horses are herding animals – it'll follow the others along.'

'Are we riding back to the railroad tracks?' the vice president's brother wanted to know.

'No. If Mickey Dent did manage to find other members of the gang, we'd find ourselves riding right toward them. We're taking a little detour, parallel to the tracks, but a few miles north.'

'How do we even know which way north is? In this storm.'

'When the wind blasts you full in the face, you're traveling north,' Ned told him. 'Now, let's quit wasting time and hit the trail.'

They started on through the darkness, Tango

having chosen the buckskin horse for himself, mounting Maria on the small paint pony. Ned and Wilson rode the two roans. Watching Wilson try to guide his horse might have been laughable under other circumstances. His face was grim; he seemed to balance himself in the saddle instead of using his knees. He rode with his back ramrod stiff, the reins sliding like slippery eels between his fingers. Wilson had been holding up pretty well to this point. Now it seemed that his dread of riding was the worst of his trying experiences. The snow had almost ceased; the wind seemed to be abating somewhat. Looking over his shoulder, Tango thought he saw a line of gray to the east. Daylight was arriving sooner than he had realized. Which was good and not so good. Anyone tracking them could easily follow the prints their horses were leaving in the hock-deep snow.

Tango eased his horse up beside Ned Chambers and said above the wind, 'Well, you've got both of your special passengers out of trouble; you'll make it.'

'All we have to do is find a trail up another four thousand feet of mountain without food, water, feed for the horses,' Ned said glumly.

'Well, that's what they pay you for, Ned,' Tango answered.

'You talk as if you're not going with us,' Ned said in amazement.

'I don't think I will be,' Tango said easily, earnestly.

'What's that?' Wilson who had drawn even with the two asked. Behind them the sky was coloring. Crimson and deep violet showed through the shifting clouds. 'You're not riding with us, Mr Tango?'

'I don't think so, sir.'

'Why? Have you got a better idea?'

'It's not better; it's a matter of duty,' Tango said as both men watched him, puzzlement on their faces.

'All right, Tango,' Ned Chambers said, 'explain yourself.'

Tango briefly turned his eyes down as a wind gust lifted snow from the ground and flung it in their faces. 'Mr Chambers here,' he told Wilson, 'had his assignment. Keeping you and Marina safe. I have only my standing orders to watch out for the railroad's interests.'

'Meaning what?' Marina who had caught up with them shouted above the wind.

'Meaning that we have a train missing and a lot of cold and angry passengers left behind. These people paid the Colorado and Eastern money to get where they were going, and they deserve to have any assistance that we can give them.'

'I don't see what you can do,' Wilson grumbled.

'Neither do I, truthfully,' Tango admitted. 'But I'm supposed to try. That's what I get paid for.'

'So, you're . . . what?' Marina asked. 'Going to chase down the train?'

'I don't think I'll have to do that,' Tango said with more confidence than he felt. 'I believe I know where the train is.'

'How could you?' Wilson asked.

When Tango answered, he was speaking to Ned. 'You know where the Northrop cut-off is, don't you?'

'What's that?' Marina asked.

Ned told her, 'It's a spur that was originally constructed to reach a town called Northrop. The only problem was that by the time the cut-off had been constructed, the town had already expired. They experienced a brief, rich run as a gold town, but the ore ran out in no time and the people scattered, leaving the Colorado & Eastern with a useless spur.

'Why Mr Tango here thinks they took the train there, you'd have to ask him. We have the two passengers they might have profited in kidnapping if they were in it for political reasons or simply had heard about Marina's half a million in jewels. And as far as we could tell from our position, they didn't even bother to rob the passengers left on board. Simply threw them from the train to stand in the weather. So, Tango. What is it you think the robbers wanted?'

'Oh, they've already got it,' Tango drawled.

'If not money . . .' Marina said.

'Oh, it's money, believe me. And they've already got it.'

'What are you talking about, Tango?' Wilson asked in exasperation.

'It's the first time I've ever heard of anyone trying it,' Tango answered. 'But I think they were after the train itself. The ransom they might demand from the railroad for its return is more than they could have gotten even if they had known about Marina's jewels. If it had been someone after you, Mr Wilson, they wouldn't have stopped looking when they did.

'No, sir, I think we've witnessed the kidnapping of an entire railroad train.'

FOUR

As the sky began to clear at mid-morning Wilson especially could see the situation they were in. Snow blanketed the ground and behind them the crimson-violet eastern sky flared brightly, hiding the disc of the rising sun. But ahead, looming prodigiously, stood the bulk of the Rocky Mountains with purple, snow-capped peaks rising to over 14,000 feet. Folded, convoluted, they were an impossible, impassible barrier.

'My God,' he muttered, 'are we to enter those!'

'Denver's at just over five thousand feet, about fifteen miles from here,' Ned answered. 'We won't be trying those high peaks, no. No man can ride up there.'

'Even so,' Wilson said shakily. 'What does that leave us from here? Another three thousand feet nearly straight up to travel. Can we do it? Can the horses do it?'

'I don't know,' Ned had to admit. 'We can drop down and follow the railroad tracks once we're well past Northrop. That's our best bet, I think.'

'A bet is right,' Wilson exclaimed. 'Without supplies we're gambling with our lives out here, aren't we?' He glanced again at the bulk and thrust of the Rockies.

'It's the only chance we have,' Ned said darkly.

'I think my little horse is almost done in already,' Marina said, patting the weary paint pony's neck. 'Isn't there some other way? Ned? Tango?'

Tango's buckskin horse shuddered under him as a gust of icy wind swept past. 'I don't think so,' Tango answered.

'But you're not going on with us, are you?' Wilson demanded.

'I can't – I have work to do. I'm heading toward the Northrop cut-off. I've got to find the missing train.'

'But there's a gang of men there, isn't there? How can you hope to accomplish anything?'

'I won't find out until I get there,' Tango said. 'Probably there's nothing I can do, but I've got to try.'

'Well, I think we should all stick together,' Marina said. Wilson instantly agreed.

'So do I,' Adam Wilson said, shuddering as he again looked at the high mountains.

'It wouldn't work,' Tango said. 'There's men with guns down there, probably a lot of them. And letting them capture Mr Wilson and rob Marina of her jewelry would undo the little we've managed to achieve.'

'Ned?' Marina asked, her eyes pleading.

'It's a reckless idea,' Ned Chambers believed.

'As dangerous as riding rough country with the winter settling in on starving, exhausted horses?' she asked pointedly.

Ned hesitated. Tango was right: to have his two charges captured would undo the little they had accomplished. But what good was it to have them free if he could not guarantee they would live to see Denver?

'Have you got a plan, Tango?'

'No. I'll have to see how things stand, if I have even guessed their scheme correctly.'

'What do you think of us tagging along?' Ned asked.

'Makes no difference to me. I suppose I'm as safe with you three as I expect to be alone. It would give me a few more guns to utilize.'

'You expect this to come to shooting?' Wilson asked stiffly.

'Oh, yes, I think I can almost guarantee you that it will come to shooting. They've gone to a lot of trouble to steal that train – they're not going to give it up easily.' Tango took a deep breath, adjusted his hat and announced, 'I'm heading down toward Northrop. Anyone else wants to come along, well I suppose you're welcome.'

They straggled on, Ned riding beside Tango. Committed to the plan of action now, Ned had a few questions. 'How will they notify the railroad what they've done?'

'Oh, I think they already have. There will have been an accomplice in Denver to notify the railroad beforehand. They didn't intend to fail. The accomplice will collect the ransom after the railroad bosses meet and discuss matters. They have to pay off, you see.

'That locomotive and the cars it's towing are worth more than the price of the steel and lumber it took to construct them. The Colorado and Eastern will lose a lot of business if it's spread around that their trains can be hijacked as easily as a stagecoach. Fares, shipping revenue on top of the millions it will cost to replace this train – when it can be done. They don't build a locomotive overnight, you know?'

'I see,' Ned said thoughtfully. 'If the train is at Northrop – which seems a logical conclusion – how in blazes do you mean to recover it?'

Tango smiled, 'That, my friend, is the part I have not figured out yet.'

'Help will be on its way from Denver.'

'Will it? The bandits chose the right place, almost precisely halfway between stations, in the middle of nowhere. Any lawmen, hired guns would have to ride just as far as you would trying to make Denver from here, through the same kind of weather. And that's assuming the people in Denver can figure out where the train is located. No, Ned, I'm not counting on any help.'

'But still you intend to tackle it? Alone.'

'That's what they pay me for,' Tango answered with a grin, but there was somberness in his eyes. Even Tango knew that he had set a nearly impossible task for himself.

'There are still passengers stranded on the tracks, back there,' Ned said, feeling for those roughly ejected from the train. 'Women and children among them.'

'First things first,' Tango replied. 'Once we have retrieved the train, we can back up along the tracks to pick them up. We'll have them warm and cozy in no time.'

Ned Chambers respected optimism, but Tango's seemed to be bordering on lunacy.

'You're crazy, Tango, you know that?'

'Give me a better idea and I'll sign on for it in an instant,' Tango said, but Ned could not, and so they rode grimly on across the barren land, the sun in their eyes, the wind at their backs.

The faded town of Northrop, when they could look down at it from a rise on the snowy bluffs above, resembled nothing more than a ghost town, which it was – weather-scoured gray buildings, shutters swinging in the wind, collapsing awnings. There soon would be nothing left to indicate that a town had ever stood there. It was a dismal and uninteresting sight.

Except for the train, which rested on the siding: a string of yellow cars and a red caboose behind a cold, dead locomotive. Now and then they saw a man moving about, but the movement seemed aimless. Whoever the men below were, they were only awaiting word that the train had been ransomed – and that could take some time.

'How'll they do it?' Ned asked in a low voice, standing beside Drew Tango as both men stood holding the reins of their weary mounts. He meant, Tango knew, how would the railroad get word to the outlaws that they were ready to pay?

'Likely send a courier on the next eastbound train, have him drop off at Northrop.'

'Why wouldn't they send a gang of railroad men in, then? Surprise the robbers?'

'I doubt all of the outlaws are in Northrop,' Tango said. 'They're probably scattered here and there in smaller camps. They'll come on the run if they hear any shooting. That might be what Stilton and his crew were doing.'

Tango continued, 'Mainly, I'd suppose there was a contingency plan already made clear to the railroad by their messenger, whoever he might have been. They'll blow up the train rather than surrender it. That would end up costing the railroad more than any ransom.'

'You're guessing that they have charges set around the train?'

'Around it, on it, under it. There's probably some dynamite waiting to be touched off if they feel like the railroad is going to try a trick,' Tango said. 'That's what I'd do. If the railroad doesn't want to play fair, the hell with them, we'll cut our losses and go on to our next bit of dirty work.'

'Surely they wouldn't,' said Wilson, who had been listening.

'Surely they would,' Tango told him. 'Do you think this gang would stop at anything? Look what they did with the passengers. Just left them standing out in a winter storm.'

There was a long silence while the four of them stood looking down into the silent valley, while the frigid wind drifted over them. Ned said:

'I wonder what happened to Frank Polk and Danny Short.'

'I doubt they'd hurt them. If they live up to their bargain, they're going to have to have a crew to run the train back to the main tracks. Probably they're locked up somewhere.'

'What are you going to do?' Marina asked. 'We're not learning anything here, and it's a toss-up if it's us or the horses that starve to death first.'

'We need to reconnoiter,' Tango said. 'Someone has to go down there and find out what's happening. Me, I suppose, since the way you people are dressed, they'd know you don't belong.'

'They'll know you don't as well,' Marina said. She stood shivering in her light jacket, her eyes concerned.

'What do you think, Ned?' Tango asked.

'I think you're right. You see, Marina, this is a very large gang, collected for this one particular job with a promise of a big payday. There's a good chance that no one man knows all of the others.'

'But,' Marina said quietly. 'There's also a chance that they do.' Her teeth were chattering now. Something had to be done and soon. 'In that case. . . .'

'In that case,' Tango said cheerfully, 'I've run out my string.' With that he swung up in the saddle, not wanting any more debate, not wanting to stand pondering his own chances and possible fate. They stood watching him as he made his way down the snowy slope, guiding the buckskin on a zigzag course toward Northrop.

'Come on,' Ned said. 'We'd better draw back a little from the edge of the bluff. Someone might spot us, and Tango's going to have a tough enough time explaining himself as it is.'

Upon reaching flat ground Tango rode directly into the deserted town, holding his head high as if he owned it. There were very few men around, as he had guessed; a skeleton crew to guard the train and perhaps to set the fuses to blow it up if Tango's theory was correct. He saw three horses tied together at a hitch rail in front of a weather-beaten building whose original function was not easily guessed, and he rode that way. He did not know if he could bluff his way through this, but he could only try. He decided to adopt a taciturn, surly manner which might be hard to bring off since inside he was quivering with fear.

He glanced at the train as he passed its length. He saw no set charges – perhaps there was none or perhaps they simply had not gotten around to it yet. These men were in no hurry; they did not expect any immediate trouble, not out here.

After tying up the buckskin Tango tramped through the mud and stepped up on to the porch. As soon as his boot touched wood the front door swung open and a man carrying a rifle and wearing a slouch hat and red-checked jacket stepped out, barring his way. Tango went on the offensive.

'Where's everybody at?' he growled. The man blinked at him. He had a lantern jaw and his sunken cheeks were peppered with whiskers. He had bulging eyes.

'Ain't that Chris Stilton's horse.'

'You got a good memory,' Tango said, striding ahead toward the door. 'Any coffee on? I've had a long cold ride.'

'From where,' the man with the rifle asked suspiciously.

Tango's voice grew more surly. 'Where do you think, from that damned way station we were posted at.'

'And you run off?'

'I don't run from anything, partner,' Tango said arrogantly. 'Stilton sent me back to see how long we were supposed to stay out there without food!'

'You boys didn't have the sense to take grub with you, it's your own fault,' the stranger said, trying for a return of insolence which he couldn't quite bring off. Tango was troubling to him, Drew could see that.

'Is there any coffee or not?' Tango asked, pushing the other's rifle barrel aside and stamping inside the dilapidated building. The stranger trailed.

'I can't make this out,' the stranger complained, removing his hat, walking to the free-standing iron stove in the center of the small room. He poured a mug of coffee and handed it to Tango. 'Mickey Dent stumbled in here this morning and said that there was some shooting going on at the way station.'

Tango sat on an old wooden chair that was held together with baling wire, sipping at his coffee. He didn't reply quickly. Of one thing he was sure, this man didn't know him from Adam. If Tango was not one of the gang, how would he know where Stilton was? If he did know, why would he ride into Northrop if he was not one of them? Tango stretched an arm and said:

'Dent's a little bit loony if you ask me – and he was at his whiskey last night. On an empty stomach. He went wandering off like a madman.'

'I've got the same opinion of the man,' the stranger said with a dry cackle and the hint of a smile. 'For some reason Russ Blair thinks highly of him, though.'

'I know,' Tango said, although he had no idea who Russ Blair was. The leader of the gang? 'I looked for Dent all along the trail, but I couldn't find him. I never thought he'd make it all this way.'

'He did. He was really raising a ruckus.' The stranger scratched at his long jaw. 'I did smell whiskey on him, now that you mention it.'

'A man that can't hold it shouldn't drink it,' Tango said. 'It's a wonder he didn't report seeing elves and dragons and such.'

'There wasn't no shooting?'

'Once Nathan and Freeman Cole went outside. Said they wanted to make sure the mechanisms of their weapons weren't froze up. They popped a few rounds into an oak tree, until Stilton told them that it wasn't such a good idea to announce ourselves. That was it.'

'Maybe that's it then. Maybe Dent was roused from a drunk by the shots and panicked.'

'I wouldn't know,' Tango said carelessly. 'He just said he was going to find Blair and the hell with the rest of us.'

'Loony,' the stranger said.

'If you ask me,' Tango replied, finishing his coffee.

For the moment Tango felt relatively secure. The older man seemed more interested in a good story than in trying to make it all fit together logically.

The old man was pacing the floor. As he passed the stove he would spit tobacco juice on it to sizzle against the black iron plate. He would look out the window intently and then walk the length of the room again. Tango decided that he would be better off leaving before further questions occurred to the man.

'I'd better see to that buckskin,' Tango said, rising. 'He's had a long run and a couple of hard nights.'

'All right. Frazier's over at the stable. He'll help you out if you need anything.'

'Good,' Tango said, walking out the door while the stranger was still absorbed in his thoughts. Tango had wanted to ask questions about this Russ Blair, but it didn't seem prudent. Outside the skies were crystal blue overhead, a few storm clouds lingering to the east, and the cutting wind had dwin-dled. Still it was cold enough as Tango walked the buckskin toward a building that could only be a stable at the end of the rutted, muddy street. One of the tall double doors stood only slightly ajar, probably to keep what warmth there was inside.

As he was walking Tango's eyes continued to survey the abandoned town and the motionless railroad cars. Nothing helpful caught his eyes until he passed a squat building with a faded sign which read only . . . RY GOODS, time and the weather having erased the rest of the lettering. The front door to this gray, flat-roofed building was closed, the shades, such as they were, drawn. In a wooden chair on the porch sat a man with a rifle between his knees, a blanket over his shoulders. He had sharp eyes which he fixed on Tango. Tango nodded and continued to make his way toward the stable as if he belonged in Northrop.

Why the guard? Tango asked. Something of value hidden there? Or perhaps the outlaws were using it as a jail. Danny Short and Frank Polk might be being held there until, if, they were needed again. It was unlikely that any of the outlaws knew how to drive a train. Were there any more of the train crew with them? Porters, con-ductors? Tango thought not. The bandits had no use for anyone else; the others would have been left beside the tracks with the unfortunate passengers.

Reaching the barn doors, Tango called out, 'Hey Frazier! Are you in there?'

'Who's it?' a sleep-heavy voice answered from inside.

'Drew Tango!' Tango had already decided to use his own name among the outlaws. He was less likely to forget what he was calling himself, and the chances of anyone recognizing the name were thin. 'I've got a horse needs some tending.'

'Come on in. I ain't stopping you,' the man named Frazier replied in the same thick voice. Frazier, it seemed, had had the right idea: sleeping out the storm in the company of the horses, who would give off plenty of body heat. Tango toed the door open, closed it most of the way with his heel and led the buckskin forward. There was a small back door, Tango noticed, also standing slightly open to allow Frazier some breath of fresh air.

A spindly-looking man with a rough-looking, mustached face that didn't quite match his form, came forward from the depths of the stable, carrying a rifle.

'Hey,' he said, suddenly suspicious, 'that's Chris Stilton's buckskin.'

'Yes, it is,' Tango said. He was not eager to repeat his story again. It was involved, and Frazier did not seem as receptive to listening to a long tale as the other man. He also might prove to be less gullible. 'I stole it from him and made my escape here,' Tango said with a straight face, hoping that Frazier would see the absurdity in that. But Frazier did not so much as crack a smile.

'I don't like this. I don't like you, whoever you are,' Frazier said stiffly. 'You might think that you're a funny man, but I'm not laughing.' He shouldered his rifle and said, 'I never seen you before. Something don't seem right here, and I intend to find out who you are.'

Tango was out of gambits. His only chance now seemed to be to draw and fire, hoping Frazier was a bad shot. That, Tango found unappealing. Frazier hesitated, but he continued to hold his rifle steady. It was then that Tango saw a flitting shadow behind the stableman. Tango talked loudly to cover up the sounds of the approaching man.

'Now, listen here, Frazier. . . .'

Then Ned Chambers, holding his rifle by the barrel, swung the stock of the Winchester against Frazier's skull and the stable man dropped his gun, went to his knees, then pitched forward on his face against the straw-strewn floor.

'What in hell are you doing here?' Tango snarled, partly with censure, partly with relief.

Ned was kneeling, removing Frazier's gunbelt. He looked up and grinned.

'You mean you aren't glad to see me?'

'Hell, yes,' Tango said, 'but what about. . . ?'

'I'll tell you later,' Ned said rising, dusting off the knees of his suit pants. 'The question is what are we going to do now?'

FIVE

Ned Chambers kept an eye on the door and on Frazier as Tango stripped down the buckskin horse, not having immediate use for it, and not wanting the animal to suffer.

'Place looks pretty deserted,' Ned commented.

'It is. Most of the outlaws have been posted out to watch for trouble arriving. Ned . . . why did you leave those two out there? With only Wilson to watch out for Marina?'

'I figure that it's the other way around,' Ned answered smiling thinly. 'She'll be looking out for him. I started thinking and decided that the only way out of here is on that train if we can get it rolling. There's no other way. I figured that whatever you were up to, you'd need some help. And I was no help to anyone sitting up on the bluff. But

69

I didn't like the idea, you can be sure of that. What's been happening down here?'

'Mickey Dent did manage to make it here, looking for help,' Tango told him. 'A crew went back to the way station to look into it. What if they track our horses back to where Wilson and Marina are waiting?'

'I don't think they will, do you?'

'No, I think the bandits will want to get back to Northrop as quickly as possible, not wanting to miss out on the pay-off. Besides, Dent is looked upon as somewhat erratic. But, Ned,' Tango said with concern, 'you never do know what will happen.'

'No, you don't, do you? Marina's going to fire three shots if she sees anyone coming. You can see for miles down the backtrail from there, you know. Then we'll have to get back up on the bluffs.' Ned's voice fell, 'Not that I know how much help we would be against a gang of men of any size.'

'We'll take the best two horses we see here,' Tango suggested. 'Give them their bits and leave them saddled and cinched so we can get out of here quickly if we have to. In the meantime. . . .'

'Yes?' Ned asked as Tango slipped out of the buckskin's stall, leaving the weary animal to munch contentedly at its hay.

70

'I think I know where Frank Polk and Danny Short are being held.'

'You don't mean it?'

'Yes, I do. How we're going to free them, I don't know, but we will need them, that's for certain, if we intend to get out of this mess.'

'We'd better try freeing them then, before any more outlaws can ride in. The ones who rode out with Dent, for example.'

'That's what I was thinking. I don't know how we're going to break them out, or what we're going to do with them afterward, but we have to try.'

'There's a lot of cunning behind this whole scheme, Tango, isn't there? Nothing you'd think your run of the mill outlaw would come up with.'

'Yes, whoever this Russ Blair is, he's canny all right.'

'Who?' Ned stared at Tango as if stunned.

'Russ Blair.'

'Where'd you hear that name?' Ned asked in apparent confusion.

'A man I met mentioned it. Why?' Ned looked confused and angry at once.

'He said that Blair was behind this?'

'As much as,' Tango answered. 'Why? Who is Russ Blair.'

Ned told him woodenly, 'Russell Blair is one of the railroad board directors in Denver.'

'I never heard of him.'

'You wouldn't in the normal course of events. Sorry, Tango, but he's a little far up the ladder for you ever to have to run across him. I was only introduced when the board called me in to discuss security for the vice-president's brother and for Lady Simpson. I hardly remember him, but the name stuck with me.'

'You're saying this is an inside job?' Tango asked.

'I'm saying it has all the characteristics of one. It had from the start – someone knowing the schedule of the train, knowing where the Northrop spur was.'

'The man must make a good salary. Why would he risk everything for a little more money?'

'A lot more money, and Tango, some men never seem to have enough.' Ned changed subjects. 'There's nothing to be done about that now – let's see what we can accomplish here, now.'

'You can't be seen walking around dressed like you are,' Tango pointed out. 'I wonder if Frazier's clothes might fit,' he said, looking at the stableman who was now beginning to stir.

'They'd be loose on me,' Ned said, 'but that

won't look unusual. When do you see a man in tailored clothes walking around out here? Let's get him undressed. I suppose we'll have to tie him and gag him. What with?'

Tango laughed. 'This is a stable, Ned. If we can't find enough rope and leather to do the job, we both ought to retire.'

Coming around slowly with what must have been a massive headache, Frazier made no sound, nor did he struggle as he was bound and hidden in the last stall. He might have figured that making any trouble could lead to another thump on the head or even death. It might have been that he was incapable of putting up a fight at that time.

Fifteen minutes later with Ned now dressed in Frazier's clothes, they walked two well-rested ponies out of the stable and headed for the alley behind the buildings as if they had business, but not especially urgent business there. The only man visible on the main street was the guard with the blanket over his shoulders. He glanced up, but at that distance he could only assume that he was seeing Frazier and the man he had directed over to the stable emerging. He wasn't concerned, nor especially curious. These were not strangers. He was taking care of his own business. Although the job he had been given left the guard sitting in the cold, it wasn't a difficult assignment. He pulled his blanket more tightly around his shoulders as the two men passed out of view.

'There's a back door,' Ned said with subdued excitement. 'If we can get in without making too much noise. . . .'

'Then what?' Tango asked with less enthusiasm. 'Where are we supposed to hide Polk and Short – assuming we don't get into shooting trouble?'

'If we can breach the door, why move them? We'll leave them where they are until it's time to call them out to work their magic on the locomotive.'

'You've got a way of making everything sound simple,' Tango growled. 'And I'm always stupid enough to believe you until we walk into complications.'

'What do you want to do?' Ned Chambers asked, mildly offended. 'Start shooting and see how many other men are hiding out around town?'

'That's one thing I've been concerned about,' Tango said. 'It stands to reason that there are more than a couple of men guarding the train, it being the purpose behind all of this. There have to be others around – but where?'

'I know where some good accommodations are,' Ned said, although Tango was already well ahead of him in his thinking. Beds, food, liquor, warmth. There was one place where the other outlaws could be secure and content. On board the train.

'And what are we supposed to do about that if it is so?' Tango asked.

'I wonder if there's any chance we could convince them that the ransom's been paid,' Ned suggested thoughtfully.

'No. There hasn't been enough time for that yet, and no one knows either of us. They won't fall for such an obvious trick.'

Ned's sigh was audible. 'Well,' he said as they halted behind the back door of the . . . RY GOODS where they assumed the locomotive engineer and his stoker were being held, 'one thing at a time.'

Ned tried the door handle and shrugged. Tango noticed that Ned Chambers's eyes continually drifted to the bluff where he had left Wilson and Marina alone. Tango stepped forward.

'Let me see, Ned,' he offered, reaching for the doorknob. Catching Ned's eyes, still fixed on the snowy bluff, he said, 'It'll be all right. She won't have to worry long.'

Which from the pessimistic Tango was somehow reassuring. Ned watched Tango turn the knob. Nothing happened, of course. The door was bound to be locked. Even so. . . .

'A normal man could pop this door with a good yank,' Tango said in a low voice despite their seeming concealment.

'And. . . ?'

'And so it makes me believe that Frank Polk and Danny Short must be bound. What do you think? Want to have a look?'

'That's what we're here for,' Ned answered uneasily.

They looked up and down the alley, then Tango put his shoulder to the door, strained briefly against it and popped it open with only a small splintering sound and the creak of rusty hinges. They let their eyes search the alleyway again, seeing no movement, hearing no rushing foot-steps. Then they stepped into the building, the ancient wooden floor complaining underfoot. The immediate temptation was to give in to the urge to call out, but they dared not. Through one of the tattered blinds they could see the silhouette of the guard in his chair out front. He had not moved, did not stir. Could he possibly be asleep in the cold out on the street? No matter; he was not roused and was apparently unaware of any sound within the old building.

They began searching the place, Tango being careful to point out old refuse, odds and ends left behind by the former tenant. There were coils of baling wire, a pitchfork with a broken handle, three or four small galvanized pails and lots of broken wooden crates, a few bottles. They made their way through the scattered mess as softly as they could.

'I thought I heard something,' Ned said, grabbing Tango's arm. Tango halted and listened too. He nodded toward a small storage room, its door closed. Halting there for a moment, they heard the sound again. It was someone murmuring muffled words. Tango put a hand to his face, indicating 'gagged'. Then, cautiously they opened the door, each man with a gun in his hand.

Against the far wall on the windowless room they saw the two railroad men sitting on the floor, each with his hands bound behind him, tied at the ankles, gags in their mouths. The engineer, Frank Polk, who had looked up with fear in his eyes, now relaxed, his gaze growing hopeful. The fireman, the young Danny Short only looked befuddled. Tango crossed to Polk and crouched down, touching a finger to his own lips, shaking his head. Polk nodded his understanding. When Tango removed the gag from the railroad man's mouth Polk began breathing harshly.

'They had that damned thing tied so tight I

thought I was going to suffocate,' Polk said.

Tango cautioned him again. 'Don't speak louder than a whisper.'

'You've come to get us out of here, haven't you?'

'That's right, but not this minute,' Tango whispered. Ned Chambers had returned to the door to act as a lookout. Polk was building up to an angry response, Tango could tell from the veins standing out in his neck. Tango cautioned Polk again.

'Frank, we have to leave you here for a little while longer. Letting you free now would start a shooting match, and we have nowhere to take you yet.' Young Danny Short was struggling with his bonds, wanting to say something as well. Tango ignored him, though he didn't feel good about it. He asked Frank Polk:

'When we do get you over to the train, how long do you think it would take you to fire it up and get ready to roll?'

'A full head of steam?' Polk frowned.

'Just enough to get us rolling, back toward the main line.'

'It would still take at least ten minutes just to get the minimum amount of pressure up,' Polk told him, 'and that won't give us much speed.'

Ten minutes – that didn't seem like a long time, but if you were in the middle of a gunfight while attempting it, it could seem like forever.

'We'll have to take what we can get,' Tango said. Ned was signaling significantly from the doorway. 'We're going to have to leave you here for a while longer. We can't get caught talking to you. We'll get you out of here, Frank, don't worry. For now I'll have to put that gag back in your mouth so no one gets wise.'

'Just don't make it so damned tight!' Polk said a little too loudly.

'Tango,' Ned said. 'Why not loosen the rope on their wrists? No one will notice that and it will give them an easier time of it when they have to get loose.'

'All right,' Tango agreed. He cautioned Polk and Danny, 'But you two have to promise me you won't try to escape on your own. It just wouldn't work.'

Even as he said that Tango was wondering about his own plan, if it could be called that – would it work? Did any of them have a chance? He thought so, as long as they tried it before the rest of the gang started arriving. There were only two armed outlaws out there that they had seen – the old man Tango had first met, and the guard in front of the store. They had no way of knowing if there were others concealed on board the train.

'I'm sorry,' Tango said, rising after he had loosened the ties on both men's wrists. 'It's just that you can't be of much help to us right now, and breaking out might get you shot down before we got started.' Polk nodded his understanding. The miserable Danny Short glared daggers at Tango, who couldn't really blame him for feeling the way he obviously did. What kind of rescue was this!

Leaving the room Tango silently closed the door. Ned Chambers paused and whispered to Tango: 'What now?'

'Now we start cleaning the place out,' Tango answered softly.

The first man to take out was the obvious one – the guard sitting on the porch, blanket around his shoulders. He might have been asleep, but whether he was or not was a matter of indifference. He was in the way and had to be removed. Through hand signs and occasional whispered words they devised a simple but workable plan.

The guard knew, or thought he knew, Tango. If he were to see Ned in Frazier's clothing he would come instantly alert. Therefore it was decided that Tango would approach the guard openly while Ned waited just inside the doorway. Once they had the man inside, they would take him down, tie and gag him and get on to more dangerous work.

It was a simple plan, but Tango knew that even the simplest of plans could blow up in your face. It didn't matter at this point in time. They had to try something.

The guard out front shivered and again tugged his blanket tighter. From around the corner of the building the blond stranger appeared, leading a horse.

'Where's Frazier?' the guard demanded, coming to his feet.

'He had some personal business to take care of,' Tango said casually. He looped the horse's reins around the hitch rail and propped one boot up on the decayed plank walk. 'I was wondering . . . did you hear that?' he asked, lowering his voice, looking intently toward the building.

'What?'

'I don't know. It sounded kind of like wood splintering.'

'Damnit!' the guard said, lurching to his feet. 'I wonder if they broke free somehow.' He had his rifle held loosely in both hands as he stared momentarily at the door. Tango offered:

'Do you want a little help?'

'I might need it,' the guard said with a grateful nod. He went to the front door, opened it an inch and tried to peer into the room. Tango gave him a hard shove and the man stumbled forward into Ned Chambers's grip. Holding the man around the neck with his arm, Ned spun the guard around so that Tango was able to tear the rifle from his hands.

The guard continued to squirm, fighting with Ned, Tango lowered the muzzle of the guard's own rifle at his belly and said softly but menacingly,

'You want to give it up or take lead?' The man stopped wriggling almost immediately, his eyes furious as he glared at Tango.

'I knew there was something wrong about you,' he said.

'Too late now,' Tango said almost cheerfully. Ned was already binding the man's hands behind his back. Tango glanced toward the window, then ripped a strip of cloth from the tattered blanket and gagged the guard. 'Let's take a walk,' Tango said, and they led the guard to the back room where he was seated facing Frank Polk and Danny Short. Ned tied the guard's feet rapidly, tightly, and told Polk and Short:

'So far, so good. You two just hang on a while longer. We'll be back.'

They slipped out the storeroom door, leaving the trainmen and the outlaw to glare at each other.

'Got a plan for the next one?' Ned panted.

'I don't think he'll give us much trouble,' Tango answered. 'Let me go first, then walk up a few minutes after I've gone in. I just hope I don't have to shoot the man.'

'So do I. We've been lucky this far, Tango, but we're stretching it thin.'

'We are, aren't we?' Tango exited the disused store, gathered the reins to his horse and walked the length of the street to where the old man stood, still peering out the window. Yes, he was waiting for someone, but who, and how soon would they get there? There was no telling and no time for indecision. Tango walked boldly to the sagging building, loosely tethered the horse, and went in. The fire in the iron stove still burned brightly, the old man still appeared worried.

'Took you long enough just to see to your horse,' the old man said, his eyes narrowing with apparent suspicion.

'Oh well; Frazier, he just couldn't stop yakking,' Tango answered.

'Frazier? He don't usually speak unless spoken to, and sometimes not even then,' the old man said, growing more wary.

'We knew each other down the back trail,' Tango said easily, pouring himself a mug of coffee.

'Where was that, exactly?'

'Exactly in someplace we don't talk about,' Tango said, adopting his surly snarl again as if he didn't appreciate anyone asking him about his past.

'I was just asking,' the old man replied. Tango was now at the window. Ned Chambers, wearing Frazier's clothing, was approaching the building, the low sunlight behind him, his hat tugged low. 'Here comes Frazier – you can ask him, seeing you're so damned curious.'

Almost hesitantly the old man approached the window. Bending down he glimpsed Ned walking toward them, leading a pony. 'All right,' the man said, lowering his rifle. 'I guess I'm starting to get a little jittery.'

'I guess you are,' Tango said with a hint of mockery.

They could hear Ned's boots clicking against the porch and Tango gestured to the old man to open the door. He did so, lowering his rifle to hold it loosely in one hand. As Ned stepped in, head lowered, the old man exclaimed: 'What's this? You ain't Frazier!'

As he stepped away from the door he felt the prodding of a blue steel revolver low on his back. Almost instantly he dropped the rifle, letting it clatter to the floor. Ned closed the door behind him. Tango spun the old man around and walked him back to one of the wooden chairs where he sagged to a seated position, his eyes wide with fright. Tango stood directly in front of him, the muzzle of his Colt leveled at the old man's chest.

'You can kill me, mister, but I'm not talking.'

'All right,' Tango said, earing back the hammer of his revolver. He was expressionless; the old man's eyes revealed terror.

'God! Don't take me serious,' the old man said. Ned was busy tying his hands behind his back. 'What do you want to know?'

'Who's on board the train?'

'Who's . . .' the man looked puzzled. He shook his head, 'No one. No one's on the train. Why would they be?'

Ned said, 'Well, it seemed like a good guess.'

'Yes, and it's also a good guess that he's lying,' Tango said.

'We don't seem to be as good at guessing as we thought,' Ned commented, tightening a knot.

'Which is it, mister?' Tango demanded. 'Are you telling the truth, or are you prepared to live out the last minutes of your life in that chair?'

'God's honest truth,' the old man said. 'There's nobody on the train. They're all posted out in small camps, waiting for whatever happens next.'

'All right,' Tango said, lowering his gun. The old man, sitting near the stove, was perspiring freely, but it was not all due to the heat it gave off. 'Where's the dynamite, then?'

'Dynamite?' Now the old man looked utterly baffled. 'What dynamite?'

'Another wrong guess,' Ned put in. 'The train isn't rigged.'

'If we take this scarecrow's word.'

'They didn't really need to take the trouble, Tango. So long as the railroad thought they were ready to go to that extreme – a threat's as good as the reality at this distance.'

'I suppose so,' Tango said. He was faintly upset that he was wrong in his conclusions, but more than a little relieved that they would not have to dismantle explosive charges before they could try to make their escape.

'Anything else?' he asked Ned. 'We've got to get going.'

'What does he know about Russ Blair?' Ned asked. Tango looked the question at the old man.

'I only seen him once, two months ago in Denver. He's the boss; that's all I know, I swear it!'

'Gag him?' Ned asked.

'There's no one left to hear him if he calls out,' Tango said with a threatening glance at the old man. 'We've taken care of the others.'

The man caught the implications. Shakily he promised, 'I won't cry out, mister. Just don't kill me!'

'You're alive and warm,' Tango said in his most menacing voice. 'You're better off than the others. Just see that you remember your promise. I'd hate to have to come back.'

'Go get the train crew, Ned,' Tango ordered. 'If we're going to make our try, now's the time.'

'Marina. . . .'

'We'll figure out some way to alert her.'

'That won't be necessary,' Lady Marina Simpson said from the doorway.

SIX

'Marina!' Ned Chambers said with astonishment. He turned and walked to her, putting his arms around her. Tango noticed that she did not pull away or seem offended. 'What are you doing here? Why did you come? It's very dangerous.'

'Probably no more dangerous than standing in the snow hour after hour,' she argued. 'I was watching you two from the bluff. Whatever you were doing you must have been successful at it. At least no shooting started. And in all that time I never saw any of the bandits slipping around near town. I told Wilson we might as well come in.'

'Did he agree?'

'After I told him I was going to anyway. He hadn't the stomach for staying out there alone. I told him to hide in the stable until I found out what I could – I hope that was a good idea.'

'Good enough,' Ned had to admit.

Tango spoke up, 'Look, Marina, we're ready to make our try now – to get the train going. Keep hold of your rifle and keep a sharp eye out. That's the most help you can be. We're going to bring the engineer and his fireman out now. Once they fire up the boiler, someone's bound to come to see what's happening. So when you see the crew in the locomotive cab, get aboard the train quickly. And keep your head down!'

'All right,' she said calmly. 'I understand.'

'This joker here,' Ned said, nodding toward their captive, 'assured us that there's no one else on board the train, but we don't know if we can trust him. While the engineer is trying to get up a head of steam, Tango and I are going to search it. Don't wander around the train until we've done that.'

'I won't,' Marina said, again without evident nervousness. 'I'll stay at a window with my rifle.'

'Good girl,' Ned said, and he took the time to hug Marina again as Tango watched, his mouth twitching.

'No time for that,' Tango said. 'Marina – get Wilson and sneak him on board. Ned and I are going to release the train crew.' They started toward the door. Tango took a moment to look back at the captured bandit.

'If you were lying about the train being empty you'll regret it, old man.'

Leaving their horses, Tango and Ned Chambers raced back toward the store where they had left Frank Polk and Danny Short. They entered through the front door, moved quickly to the storeroom and untied the engineer and the fireman. Neither could rise by himself after sitting bound for so long. They were assisted to their feet and stood against the wall, breathing deeply, shaking their limbs to aid the circulation. Danny Short was wincing, and Tango knew what that was – invariably they would feel the pins and needles of returning blood.

The captured guard sat watching them bleakly. For a single moment he had had the idea that his men were returning to free him, but that hope had faded to grim acceptance of the reality.

'Are you men up to firing up that locomotive?' Ned asked after a few minutes.

'I don't know, but now's the time we have to try, isn't it?' Frank Polk said, rubbing his calf muscle.

'It is. Let's get to it,' Tango said with subdued excitement. Because if they did not get the locomotive moving, everything that had gone before was nothing more than a waste of their time. They moved toward the front door, Frank Polk still limping heavily. Tango peered out, saw no one.

'Where's Marina?' Ned asked in a whisper.

'If I know her, she's right where she's supposed to be. On board the train.'

In a group they started across the muddy street toward the train.

'Hold it right there!' someone cried and they turned to find themselves facing the old man. He had a rifle, and it was aimed at them.

'I thought you could tie a knot,' Tango hissed at Ned. Before Ned could respond, the old man fired off his first shot. The bullet tagged Frank Polk in the thigh, and he half-spun around before dropping to the ground. Tango had his Colt out, ready to return fire.

It wasn't necessary. A rifle spoke from the window of the nearest railroad car and they saw the old man fold up on the street. Smoke curled from the barrel of the Winchester Marina Simpson held.

'Get out of the open!' she yelled at them, and they hurried on toward the train. Also hastening toward it from the end of the street, was Adam Wilson. He had shed his coat in the warm stable and loosened his tie. Now, his face beet red, he scurried toward the train. Danny Short, who had struck them as ineffectual, crouched and shouldered Frank Polk, carrying him to the locomotive.

Tango and Ned hoisted the engineer up into the cab. Frank was bleeding heavily from his leg wound. Tango whipped off his scarf to apply a crude tourniquet. Beside him, Ned asked:

'What do we do now? Without an engineer.'

'I can drive it,' Danny Short volunteered, 'as long as I've got Frank here to coach me.' Frank, in terrific pain, managed to nod. 'I'll need a fireman though, and now,' Danny said.

'What's that require?' Wilson asked from the iron steps where he was clinging on.

'Jamming as much wood into the firebox as it will hold, and then scrambling up into the tender to bring down as much additional fuel as you can. You have to keep moving.'

'I can do that,' Adam Wilson said, surprising them. He was rolling up his shirtsleeves. 'Just show me how to get the fire in the box started.'

'Here they come!' Ned shouted, for from the corner of his eye he had seen a body of horsemen emerging from the pine forest. Bullets began to sing around them, striking iron plate and whining off into the distance. They heard Marina's rifle crack once and saw a man on a sorrel horse fall from the saddle.

'You'd better get back there with her,' Tango said.

'What about you?'

'I'm staying here for awhile,' Tango said, ducking late, uselessly, as a rifle bullet ricocheted off the steel canopy of the locomotive. Ned nodded and left, scrambling up across the tender, logs and split wood rolling from under his boots as he clawed his way toward the passenger cars, bullets flying around him.

He rolled roughly down to the platform behind the tender and entered the passenger car, where a resolute Marina Simpson had perched on a seat, her rifle at the ready. She looked beautiful, her eyes flashing, one dark curl which had escaped from its pins falling across her forehead.

'I thought I told you to stay down.' Ned panted, seating himself on the bench across the aisle.

'That wouldn't have done us much good, would it?' she snapped. As she spoke the last words, she squinted along her sights and fired off another round, black acrid smoke swirling past them, hanging heavily against the ceiling.

'I think I missed him,' she said, jacking a fresh round into the Winchester's receiver. 'I shouldn't have. We'd better quit talking.'

Ned agreed and dropped his own window to watch for movement on his side of the train. In the cab of the locomotive Drew Tango was firing his own rifle to some effect. Three men, riding nearly abreast, emerged from the depths of the pine woods, their guns blazing wildly. Tango's own platform for shooting was much steadier than the back of a galloping horse, and he picked off two of the men, causing the last to have an abrupt change of heart. The bandit, riding a gray horse, wheeled around and raced for the woods. Tango's rifle sent him a parting message of warning.

Beside him, Tango watched as Danny Short tried rapidly, if inexpertly, to follow Frank Polk's instructions on the use of the various valves and the reading of the seemingly complex cluster of round gauges on the flat control dash of the engine.

'Just keep watching the pressure gauge,' Frank commanded. His voice was not loud. He sat sagging against the floor of the cab, his bloody leg outstretched, his other tucked beneath him. He was quite pale, and his orders came around between ragged puffs of breath.

It was growing hot in the cab, a good sign. Adam Wilson had bent to his task with more vigor than Tango had expected. He, too, was working to save his life. With the break in the attack, Tango thought he should try to help Wilson, who had recently slipped from atop the tender, bringing down a shower of split logs with him. Before he could move that way, however, a fresh group of bandits broke from the woods and Tango settled in to do what he did best, shooting the attackers from their saddles.

Now and then he could hear Frank Polk gasping out instructions, hear him demand raggedly, 'What's the pressure in that boiler, Danny? Got oil pressure?' and various other words he could not understand, so muffled with pain were they. Danny Short seldom shifted his eyes from the big red arrow of the boiler's pressure gauge which held all of their hopes. Now and then Danny would glance at Wilson, who was still working as hard as he could, but was obviously faltering as he continued with the unaccustomed labor.

'Here they come again,' Danny Short called out as a bullet from the far side of the train sang wickedly through the cab, striking iron. In a crouch, Tango went to that side, positioning himself on a knee. Peering over the skirt of the cab he saw four men in a file riding past the train, rear to front. Tango heard Ned's rifle bark, saw a man somersault from his pinto pony and lie sprawled, unmoving against the earth. Why they had chosen to attack in that manner, Tango couldn't guess, but the bandits had exposed themselves as if they were figures in a shooting gallery. Tango shot the first man in the line, and that one veered toward the trees, holding his chest. Tango waited while the next man rode into his sight and watched with satisfaction as that one tumbled from his saddle. The next man he missed as he doubled up in the saddle. Ned had tagged him first. Slumped over his horse's withers, this one also dashed for the forest verge, although Tango doubted he would make it that far.

'We got it!' Danny Short shouted out triumphantly. 'The needle just hit the green line!'

'Don't waste time bragging about it,' Frank Polk moaned miserably. 'Kick off the brake and find reverse.'

The brake, a steel lever stretching up four feet into the cab, with a clasp handle to release it, took the efforts of both Danny Short and Tango to operate. With a massive exhalation of steam the locomotive came to life, the four huge drive-wheels slipping, spinning, grabbing for purchase. And then slowly, heavily, the train began to move backward. They were followed by rifle fire from the woods, but as they gained speed and distance these shots became few and futile.

'Watch your speed!' Frank Polk warned. 'You'll buckle the couplings on the curve if you're not careful. These things aren't built for backward speed.'

Then he closed his eyes and said nothing else as the train rumbled and rattled in reverse along the long stretch of the cut-off.

'What do I do now?' Adam Wilson asked. He was standing against the skirt, holding his heart. Danny Short, who made his living as a fireman, said with some disparagement, 'Just keep on doing what you're doing – faster if possible. When we start running forwards, flat out, we are going to need a lot of speed if we're going to leave the gang behind.'

Tango placed his rifle aside. 'I'll help you, Wilson. Do you want to stoke the boiler or get up top of the tender and throw the wood down?'

'If you could' – Wilson said with weary appreciation – 'get up on the tender. It's the climbing up and down that's defeating me.'

And weight, and age, and too many Washington DC parties and lack of exercise, Tango thought, but did not say. The man had done his best at a crucial moment; he did not deserve criticism.

The train rolled along more smoothly now.

Tango continually looked back for approaching riders, but even at the moderate speed of the backing locomotive, a man would have to be mad to pursue it on horseback.

As the train huffed along steadily if not comfortably, Ned Chambers and Marina stood on the rear deck of the caboose. Ned had searched the sleeping berths along the way. There was no sign of any concealed bandits. The land, raw, patched with snow and void of any structures, slid away beneath their view.

'I still don't see the abandoned passengers,' Marina said, as she stood sheltered beneath Ned's arm.

'Let's hope there are survivors,' Ned commented.

'Oh, Ned, don't say that!'

'Well, it could be, you know.'

'I'm sure they'll be all right,' Marina said, 'I still can't believe the indifference to human suffering those bandits showed leaving them out in the storm all night.'

Ned nodded, thinking about the calculated cruelty to men women and children. He knew that Marina wanted to hear positive words, and so he told her, 'Well, the storm broke early this morning. And the passengers had the wood from the bonfire the bandits used to stop the train. They would have reignited it and kept warm in that way.'

'I think so,' Marina said. Yet doubt was lingering in her eyes. 'I still can't see them. How far back would you think they were?'

'At least five miles at a guess – surely we rode that far last night.'

'I wonder how fast we're traveling – it's difficult to tell.'

'We'll be there soon,' Ned said, letting his eyes meet hers, lingering there. 'Then we hurry them all on board, out of the cold, and off we go.' He tried speaking cheerfully, but in his own heart he was not so sure that everything would work out so easily.

'Look,' Marina said, suddenly raising a pointing finger. 'There they are – at least some of them.'

'It looks like a few men started walking the rails trying to find help,' Ned said, squinting into the distance. 'I'd better go up front and tell them to slow the train.'

When Danny Short brought the train to a rather shaky halt, Frank Polk stuttered a few words in a weak voice. 'Damn, boy, release some steam. You're trying to make the old horse stop and go at the same time!' He was feverish now, and much weaker from the loss of blood.

99

'We'd better get him into a berth,' Tango said. 'Danny, will you be all right on your own?'

'Just get Frank to where he'll be comfortable.'

Before that could be accomplished a party of five men arrived at the locomotive – men sent out looking for help for the stranded passengers. The man at the front of the group was a scarfaced, small-eyed man of forty or so. His face was red with rage.

'It took you people long enough,' he bellowed, grabbing the iron rail to climb up on the steps leading to the cab.

Tango started to snap back, but Ned said smoothly, 'We're here now. That's all that matters.'

'Is it! Maybe to you, but I was due in Denver last night. I am James Tittle of the Range West Mining Company. My corporation was supposed to make a bid on a few of the smaller mines this morning. If we've lost out on that, there will be hell to pay. Hell to pay!'

In his even voice, Ned instructed Tittle and the others, 'Climb aboard and rest your feet, men. We'll be heading for Denver in a matter of minutes.'

'I won't forget this,' Tittle said. The man was nearly apoplectic. He lowered himself to the ground and stomped off toward the passenger cars.

'We've been hearing that for the last two miles,' a second member of the group said. He was a younger man, well set-up, wearing a thin dark mustache. 'My name's Austin Porter. Personally I'd like to thank you men for getting here at all. I have no idea what you've been through – maybe you'll tell us when you have the time. Do you need some help moving the engineer to the train? I can tell he's badly hurt.'

'I'd appreciate it if you don't mind,' Ned Chambers said with a nod. Ned and Porter lowered Frank Polk to the arms of two of the other men and he was taken off to a sleeping car where Ned and Marina tucked him into a bed despite his protests.

'The kid needs some help,' Frank said, his head rolling back and forth on his pillow. 'Danny can't . . . tell him we'll need water for the boiler. Take her on to the siding at Big Bend. They'll have. . . .'

Then Frank, who had been clenching the sheets, released his grip and fell silent. Marina looked at Ned with concern.

'He's alive,' Ned told her. 'Just exhausted.'

The train jerked just then beneath their feet. Danny Short was continuing his backward run toward the stranded passengers.

'Remember to tell him what Polk said about Big

Bend,' Marina said, clinging to Ned's shirtsleeve. 'We have to have water, I know. If we get stranded again, I might start losing my composure.'

'You're holding up fine,' Ned said truthfully. 'No one could have done better. I'll tell Danny about Big Bend when the train stops again.'

He kissed her on the forehead, amazed at how far their relationship had come since their first meeting. Trouble has a way of driving people apart or bringing them together. It all depends on what the people involved are made out of.

Marina Simpson was made of stern stuff.

Ned only hoped that he could continue to keep her safe. He had no confidence that their troubles were over. The train rumbled clumsily on.

SEVEN

'I don't think I've ever been this tired in my life,' Adam Wilson was saying. He had buttoned his collar and reattached his tie, though he had not put a jacket on, when the group sat down to a meal at the small dining table as the train rolled on across the plains. There was still a smudge on his forehead which he must have been aware of, but seemed to wear as a badge of honor.

The meal was of plain fare. The train crew had served apples, ham, cheese and bread to all on board. The first-class passengers got nothing special on this day. Probably the dining crew, stranded along with the passengers overnight, had voted to make the simplest meal possible, serve it quickly and eat themselves. No one could blame them.

Lady Simpson had retrieved a pink chiffon dress from her berth and wore that, having taken the time to pin her dark hair on top of her head once again. She wore no jewelry on this day. Ned Chambers had brushed his coat and pants as well as he could; he figured he looked at least halfway respectable. Joining them was the younger man with the thin mustache who had introduced himself as Austin Porter.

Wilson was telling them, 'It was quite remarkable, really. I thought I was about to faint from the heat of the firebox when that rude man we met – James Tittle – clambered forward, removed his jacket and announced that he was taking over.'

'Maybe we misjudged him,' Ned commented, sipping at his red wine.

'He's a single-minded sort. He wants to get to Denver, and quickly. He said he was going to get there or 'bust a gut trying',' Wilson told them. 'And the way he fell to work on the wood pile, I think he might just to that.'

'How's Danny doing?' Ned asked.

'I couldn't judge, but from the looks of things he's got everything under control.'

'I've got to get up there and relieve Tango as soon as I've finished my meal,' Ned said.

'Would you?' Wilson asked. 'I have to admit it:

I'm just not up to that sort of work any more.'

'I take it you are in the trades?' Austin Porter who had not been introduced when he seated himself asked.

'In a manner of speaking . . .' Wilson began. Marina cut in.

'This is Adam Wilson, the brother of Mr Henry Wilson, the Vice-President of the United States.'

'You don't say?' Porter said, 'I am happy to make your acquaintance.'

'I take no credit for my brother's success,' Wilson replied modestly, though it was apparent that he enjoyed his position.

'And this is Lady Simpson,' Ned said, his eyes lingering on Marina as she smiled faintly and nodded to Porter.

'Two famous individuals at the table,' Porter said, lifting his own wine glass.

'Me famous?' Marina laughed. 'My husband enjoyed some celebrity, but not I.'

'Perhaps not in your own eyes,' Porter said, 'but, may I speak with you later, Lady Simpson? You see, I am by occupation, a newspaper editor, and I think my readers might be fascinated in hearing of your experiences.'

Marina hesitated, glanced at Ned and answered. 'I must demur, Mr Porter. I can't see any reason for anyone to be interested in my rather ordinary life and times.' She kept her eyes on Ned as she spoke, seeming to be asking him if they should reveal the plot they thought they had uncovered.

'Well, another time,' Porter said easily. 'What about you, Mr Wilson? Surely you could not object to an interview.'

'I don't object,' Wilson said, 'but your request is untimely. I have certain business to conduct in Denver which is better left to discretion at this time.'

'Ah, well,' Porter said with a good-natured smile, 'I suppose then, it's back to Denver and reporting more wonders like Mrs Donohue's cow giving birth to triplets.'

Before the others were finished with their meal, Ned rose. He was feeling some guilt about leaving Tango out there lugging wood while he dined. Besides, he had not yet relayed Frank Polk's message about halting for water at Big Bend.

Walking through the passenger cars he saw a mostly contented group. Their anger at the rail-road, if any, had been soothed by food and warmth. They were asleep for the most part, feeling themselves far away from the trouble of the day before.

Ned hoped that they were correct. He had no

way of knowing if the train robbers might continue with their scheme at any given chance – which might or might not be Big Bend. The water stop was not something the average robber would think of, but it was a railroad man who was running the show.

Russell Blair.

Ned really knew nothing about the big man with the reddish mustache and loose, almost slovenly body. They had met only a handful of times. Was his plot an angry striking out at the Colorado & Eastern for some real or imagined grudge, or was cash money – a lot of it – his only aim?

'About time,' was Tango's welcome when Ned Chambers slipped around the corner of the fuel tender to join him in the locomotive cab. 'I'm sweating my face off while you're dining on steaks and sipping champagne.'

'It wasn't quite that fancy,' Ned answered with a grin. He removed his coat. 'Anyway, I'm here now.'

'None too soon for me,' Tango said, leaning back against the skirt of the cab. Danny Short glanced around at him, and Tango told him, 'Kid, you must have a lot of wiry muscle under that shirt to have done this for years as you have.'

Danny just grinned and shook his head.

'Move aside,' James Tittle ordered, 'you're

blocking the firebox.'

Tittle had an armload of wood. His face was smudged, his shirt had ripped out at the shoulder seam. Ned moved away. 'You want me up in the tender or down here?' he asked.

'Do whatever you think you can do best,' Tittle snapped. 'I'm getting this train to Denver if I have to pack it on my back.'

'You still have hopes of consolidating those small gold claims?'

'Mister,' Tittle said, straightening up, his eyes flashing, 'I *have* to do it. I've got some unforgiving partners.'

Ned slipped up to where Danny stood at the controls, his cap tugged low, peering along the long silver rails. 'Frank Polk said to watch your water level. He said to tell you that you should use the Big Bend siding to fill the boiler.'

'All right,' Danny answered without looking at Ned. All of the young man's attention was on gauges and rail conditions. He seemed determined to succeed. 'You know, mister, this is Frank Polk's engine, but one day I'll have one of my own.'

'You like this life?'

'There couldn't be none better. On an open throttle rolling across the wide lands from station to station . . . there ain't no better life.'

Ned said, 'I'm sure you'll make it. This run is bound to impress the bosses.'

'Maybe – you're a railroad detective, aren't you?'

'Yes, I am.'

'Maybe if you do ever meet with the higher-ups . . .' he turned sincere, blue eyes on Ned, 'you could drop a word or two in my favor.'

'I will, and I'm sure Frank will.' Ned nodded goodbye to Tango as he waved a hand and stepped to the tender's catwalk, then asked Danny: 'How far is Big Bend, anyway?'

'I'd say ten miles – make that fifteen minutes' traveling time.'

'Coming up fast.'

'Yes, sir,' said Danny who had obviously been doing his own thinking. 'Let's just hope there's no one there to meet us.'

When Tango reached the dining car only Adam Wilson remained at the table. He looked haggard and Tango himself felt little better. He knew he would stiffen up as time rolled on. Wilson looked up from his wine and nodded.

'Gave you a lunch break, did they?'

'Yes, and I can use it,' Tango said, sliding into a chair.

'I always thought of myself as relatively fit – until

109

I got out here,' Wilson said with a faint smile.

'If it makes you feel any better, I had a rough time of it myself,' Tango admitted. 'I don't know how those men can do that all day, every day.'

'I suppose it's a matter of what you're used to,' Wilson said, passing the wine bottle to Tango.

'I suppose . . .' Tango said, his thoughts trailing off. From the corner of his eye he had seen a stealthy figure moving down the corridor toward the berths. 'Where's Lady Simpson?'

'Lady Simpson?' Wilson's high brow furrowed. 'I think she said something about needing to get some rest. I don't blame her. . . .' Tango never heard the rest of Adam Wilson's words. He was up and out of his chair, tossing his napkin on to the table, drawing his Colt. The man, whoever it was, had slipped into one of the sleeping cars. Tango paused. Then he heard it, a small muffled complaint from behind a closed door and he strode that way.

Now the muted voice was louder, and it was a woman's voice. Tango shouldered the locked door once and then turned and kicked it in. A man was bent over Marina, holding a pillow over her face. Her feet kicked, her head thrashed. The man, who wore a suit and had a thin mustache continued to press down.

The assailant's face turned toward Tango, his eyes wide. He muttered a curse and turned toward Drew Tango, but Tango was to him in one stride, and he chopped down on the man's skull with his pistol barrel. The man didn't go down at once; he spun away and ducked, narrowly avoiding a second blow, this one from Tango's empty left fist. Marina had thrown the pillow off her face and she sat up in bed, her mouth open as if to scream, but no sound emerged. Her dark hair was in a tangle, her eyes furious.

'He was after my jewelry,' she said as Tango moved in, drove his gun barrel into the thug's wind, and when he doubled up, Tango brought up a knee to the thief's face, breaking nose-bone and teeth. The man staggered back against the wall, his face streaming blood.

'Who is he?' Tango asked, holding his gun steady on the quivering would-be robber.

'He called himself Austin Porter,' Marina panted, holding her throat. 'He told us he was a newspaper man. He came in here to ask for a story about my jewels – he said. Then things got rough.'

'So you're Porter,' Tango said. The name, if not the face, was familiar to the railroad detective. Porter had been working the rails for some time, flattering wealthy men and women with his story of being a newspaper editor, charming them into revealing more than they would have with a promise of getting their names in the newspaper. 'Let's go!'

'By whose authority,' Porter demanded, willing to play it out to the end. Tango drew back the hammer of his revolver.

'By the authority of Colonel Samuel Colt,' Tango said grimly.

'This is all a mistake,' Porter said, wiping his bloody chin with the back of his hand.

'I'd say so,' Tango said. 'Get out into the corridor – I'd do it now if I were you.'

Porter still hesitated, so Tango grabbed him by the arm and spun him around before Porter could get any more ideas. Shoving the thief out into the corridor, Tango marched him at gunpoint to the rear platform.

'Where are we going? What do you mean to do with me?' Porter squeaked as Tango nudged him forward with the muzzle of his revolver.

'Open the door!' Tango commanded and Porter looked at the tall blond man with genuine fear.

'Why?'

'Open the damned door!' Tango repeated, and shakily Porter did so. A gust of freezing wind swept

through the narrow corridor. Tango shoved Porter
out on to the iron platform.

'What now?' Porter asked, shivering in his light
jacket.

'Now start looking for a soft spot, a bank of
snow, because you're going to jump.'

Porter's eyes went wide with horror. 'At this
speed! Look, give me a break, won't you?'

'You've already gotten one,' Tango replied.
Because if Ned Chambers had caught Porter
attacking Marina, Tango had no doubt that Ned
would have killed him.

'A man out here – in this weather – probably
with a broken leg. . . .' Porter pleaded.

'Always has a chance,' Tango said. 'But don't
ever hop the Colorado and Eastern again, because
I'd take that personal.'

Then, with Porter cringing, beginning to weep,
Tango stepped toward him, gripped the shoulder
of his coat, turned the robber, and hurled him
from the platform. Tango didn't know if the man
had found a soft spot to land on or not, and he
didn't care much. He turned, shut the door
against the force of the wind and walked back
toward the dining car. As he passed Marina's room
he saw her peering out of the door. She smiled
gamely at him and whispered:

'Thank you.' Without another word she closed the door.

Adam Wilson was still at the table. He glanced up curiously at Tango, but did not ask questions. He had already learned that in the West it is not considered good form to ask a lot of those.

'Sorry, Tango. I seem to have been nibbling away at the rest of the food. There's nothing left but an apple and half a bottle of wine. Do you want me to call the servers?'

'No – those men have already done their best. They'll be trying to relax now. You could pass that wine bottle over, though.'

The train was slowing. Everyone on board could feel it. A few passengers grew anxious, staring out the windows to see what new trouble might be arriving. Tango took it upon himself to stand in the front of the cars and tell everyone:

'It's nothing to worry about, folks, we just need some water for the boiler from the tank here. We'll be rolling again in a few minutes.'

Or so he hoped.

The mountains loomed tall above the lonely station of Big Bend. It was hard to say how a man could live here, on his own, for any length of time, but the manager, a spindly-thin man named

Dingle, seemed to be in high spirits – maybe that was because he was seeing human faces for the first time in weeks.

The train had sort of jerk-jumped to a halt in the vicinity of the water tower. Danny Short looked abashed, as if he could imagine what Frank Polk was saying about the ragged halt. He made an apology to Tango, but Drew just shrugged.

'There aren't many jobs learned on the first day, Danny.'

'No, I guess not. But I've been watching Frank Polk for nearly a year – it's funny how he can make everything look so easy, and when I try the same thing, I feel like a fumbling fool.'

'You got us this far,' Tango smiled.

Even as he said that, both men stood looking up from the station to the mountains, seeing where the tank-town got its name. The rails began to rise and curl in a sweeping arc across the mountain-side. Tango knew that Denver was still 3,000 feet above them, so he estimated the Big Bend rise to be about that. A train losing its head of steam on the upgrade would find itself in real trouble. The same thought seemed to shadow Danny Short's eyes as he looked toward the peaks. Tango felt some trepidation, but Danny was responsible for getting that massive construction of wood, iron and steel up it.

'Are you up to it, Danny?'

'I suppose I'd better be,' Danny said hesitantly. 'I was thinking – if ever anyone started a rockslide up there – it would just be too bad for us, wouldn't it?'

Dingle who had not been listening approached them and told Danny: 'Just open that throttle and trust the machine you're driving, Danny. One thing you don't have to worry about,' he added with dry humor, 'is using the brake.'

Dingle laughed drily and then went to tend to business. He clambered up the steps of the tall water tank and expertly worked the filler spout toward the boiler input, which he had already opened with a special tool.

Danny Short watched the old man clamber around with amazing spryness. 'How is Frank?' he asked.

'We moved him back to the caboose. He's doing fine,' Tango said, but to Danny's obvious disappointment added, 'but he won't be back to work any time soon.'

'I wish he could help me out,' Danny Short said nervously.

'So do we all,' Tango answered. 'But you're the man now, Danny. Take what you've learned from

Frank and listen to Dingle's advice. You'll be fine.'

Danny nodded, looking up at the silver ribbons disappearing among the jagged, snow-touched outcroppings. 'I used to wonder why so many old-time railroad men drank so much,' he said. 'Now I think I understand.'

Dingle was finished filling the boiler. Fifty gallons of surplus water washed over the locomotive as he raised the filler spout and secured it.

'Just get us up there,' Tango said. 'The train's pulled that grade a hundred times before. You're riding a well-trained beast, just let it do what it knows best.'

'Sounds good,' Danny said doubtfully. Uncertainty still dwelt behind his eyes. Tango slapped Danny on the shoulder and sauntered back toward the train. Standing in the shade of the water-stop's awning was a dismal-looking young man with broad shoulders, a square face and an odd half-sprouted mustache. It was Tango's job to know who he was, so he started that way.

'Looking for something?' Tango asked.

'Me?' The younger man turned toward him, startled. 'A way out of here, I guess. I was hoping to hop a freight. This one is all passenger cars. That makes it tough.'

'It does,' Tango agreed expressionlessly. He did

not add that it was a part of his job to toss off any hobos he might encounter. Tango thought briefly of Wilson, Ned Chambers and himself laboring as firemen through the day and overnight. He looked appraisingly at the big kid.

'You ever done any work for a living?' he asked and the kid laughed out loud.

'Mister, that's all I've done since I was six or seven. I was down in a coalmine before I was twelve. I've worked at a sawmill, I've pulled stumps, dug water wells, bucked hay – just about anything you can name, but there's no work left to do where I come from. I heard that in Denver the mines are hiring anyone who can sign his name and carry a shovel. That's why I'm trying to get there any way that I can.'

'All right – my name's Drew Tango, and I'm going to find a way for you to work your way to Denver. Go to the locomotive cab, you'll find a man called Danny Short there. Tell him I sent you and that you're the new fireman if he wants you. Danny will show you what to do.'

The big kid's grin was expansive. 'My name's Tom Pelt, and I thank you, Mr Tango.' He thrust out a thick hand which Tango shook. He was as thankful to have found Pelt as Pelt was to have a job. Tango had had enough of stoking the firebox.

He could work, did work, but the heaviest implement he was used to rode in his holster.

'What's up?' Ned Chambers asked striding up to join Tango.

'I found us a fireman. Kid named Pelt.'

'Good,' Ned said, stretching out his own weary back. 'Wilson could barely get out of bed this morning. I wasn't a lot better.'

Tango noted that Ned smelled faintly of lilac powder this morning, and he didn't think he had put it on himself. He grinned at Ned. 'Everything seems to be going well – at last.'

Then it began to snow again.

EIGHT

Ned Chambers eyed the skies with unhappy speculation. The peaks of the mountains were already concealed by dark clouds. The silver rails climbing toward the pinnacle of the Big Bend grade vanished in the jumbled darkness.

'We can't wait for it to clear,' Ned said.

'No,' Tango agreed. They did not know if they were still being pursued by the bandits. To lie over for another day could prove deadly. Besides, he did not think that the passengers, men like the brusque James Tittle, would stand for it.

'What about Danny – it looks like a wicked climb for the train,' Ned said, studying the rails which crossed a pair of tall trestles and then thrust their way skyward.

'How's Frank Polk doing?' Tango asked. 'Any

chance he could help?'

'He looks stronger, but his leg is inflamed. He can hardly stand up; he shouldn't be out in this weather.'

'Then Danny's our man,' Tango shrugged. 'We have to leave it all to him.'

Danny, when Tango visited him in the cab, did not look frightened, but there was an incredible tenseness about him as he studied the skies where snow had begun to fall heavily. Danny was wearing a buffalo-skin coat and a woolly cap with earflaps. He looked suddenly older. Behind Tango, Tom Pelt was stoking the firebox with strong, even strokes. 'What do you think, Danny?' Tango asked.

'Well, I wish this storm hadn't set in, but I've just got to give the iron horse its head and keep the firebox hot,' he said with a glance at Tom Pelt, who worked on, paying no attention to the conversation. 'Hell, we can still make Denver only a day late,' Danny said, brightening. 'How's Frank?'

'They tell me he's doing better,' Tango replied. He rested a hand on Danny's shoulder. 'Get us rolling, Dan – they'll have to give you your own train after this.'

Danny brightened at that thought, then frowned again as he turned his attention to the pressure gauge. Tango slipped from the cab and made his way back to the passenger cars.

Minutes later they were in motion again, Tango saw Dingle, a rather sad figure of a man, lifting a hand to them as the train rolled out of the watering stop.

The snows fell.

The snow came down in faltering showers at first, sticking to the granite boulders at the side of the roadbed, then sliding away down their surface. As the skies darkened and a deep-voiced rumble of thunder rolled down from the highlands, the snow increased, falling in wind-blown flurries. The train was buffeted from side to side as the locomotive was guided up the long incline.

Tango heard one woman exclaim: 'Why are we traveling on through this – look how deep the canyon below us is!'

'To get to Denver,' the gloomy James Tittle who was sitting two rows away snapped. 'That's where we're all trying to go, isn't it?' He turned his small eyes on Tango and asked, 'Have you seen that Austin Porter around?'

'Not recently,' Tango answered.

'Damn man was going to write an article about me and the mine properties I'm here to acquire – good publicity for the company, he says.'

'If I see him, I'll remind him,' Tango said, wondering what sort of trickery Porter had been planning to work on Tittle.

Many of the passengers peered out the windows of the train at the snow-covered canyon that seemed to fall farther away with each minute. Others remained huddled in blankets away from the window as if afraid to look out. Tango wondered briefly at the efforts of the men who had blasted, dug and hauled away the stone on the flank of the mountain to construct the rail line, and was glad he had not been among them. There was eight to ten feet of solid bedrock supporting the rails. To one side there was nothing but sheer, rising cliff, to the other a drop of nearly 3,000 feet. Any misstep by a worker would have been fatal. Likely no one would have ever tried to retrieve the bodies. Skeletons must have littered the canyon floor, of man and mule alike.

The wind rocked the coaches again and Tango began to feel a little uneasy himself. Now the windows revealed nothing but white gloom; only at intervals would the depths of the gaping canyon appear. The train rolled on. Tango was more than relieved now that he had made the decision to take on that young bull, Tom Pelt, to attend to the stoking tasks. It must have been frigid out there even with the blast furnace heat of the firebox.

Tango rapped on Marina's door and was summoned in by Ned Chambers. Both seemed a little flushed.

'Well?' Ned asked, 'Are we going to make it?'

'Hope so – it'll be our fault if the train stalls out on the grade, you know. We were the ones pushing Danny to take it up the mountain.'

'Well,' Ned said with a faint smile, 'They can't do much but fire us.'

'Assuming we were to live that long,' Tango answered. 'You know, if they were to lose steam we'd be stalled on the tracks maybe for days, until the storm lets up.'

'You have a cheerful outlook today,' Marina said. The words were no sooner out of her mouth than they felt trouble shudder through the length of the train.

'Rockslide?' Ned asked, instantly to his feet.

'Maybe, but we're still moving. Slowly, but we're moving.'

'No more than a walking speed,' Ned said, reaching for coat and gloves. 'Let's see what the trouble is, Tango.'

They saw it before they had even clambered up into the cab of the locomotive. Snow, covering the tracks, had briefly melted and then refrozen there. There was ice glazing the rails for as far ahead as

124

they could see through the swirling snow. Tango and Ned had approached the locomotive with extreme caution. Not three feet behind them the edge of the cliff fell away into the terrible depths of the long canyon. Tango forced himself to pretend that the drop-off did not exist. He did not look that way, but clung to every handhold the locomotive had to offer. Even with gloves on he could still feel the incongruous heat of the boiler. There were inches of snow atop the railroad cars, none at all on the locomotive where snowflakes hissed away in seconds.

The locomotive was still moving when they reached it, or rather was trying to move, as the four huge drive wheels spun, clawed for purchase and then slid dangerously down-slope. If the train ever started sledding that way it would be more than disastrous. There would be no way of slowing the iron behemoth with its cargo of living people.

Tango gripped an iron rail beside the steps and swung up into the cab where Danny Short, his face pale and drawn, worked at the controls.

'What's happening, Danny?' Tango asked although he had already diagnosed the problem.

'Ice,' Danny said with a tragic expression.

'What can we do?'

'I don't know. I remember Frank telling me

about something like this. They shoveled cinders out of the firebox and spread them along the rails . . . and *sand*!' Danny said, remembering. 'In the side-boxes of the caboose there should be hundreds of pounds of sand. The wheels can find purchase with that on the rails.'

'I'll fill these buckets with embers,' Tom Pelt said. He did not look frightened, only determined. He still wore no coat. Working so close to the firebox, he had not needed one, Tango supposed. 'I'll scatter coals along the tracks if you gents can find some men to help you haul sand forward.'

'The brakeman, Giles,' Danny said, 'he'll help. He's in the caboose with Frank. Maybe some of the serving crew, but I don't know about them.'

'It'll be tough to find any volunteers among the passengers,' Ned said.

They knew what he meant. Tiptoeing along the narrow ribbon of flat ground between the train and the maw of the gorge with a hundred-pound sack of sand on your shoulder was hardly an appealing idea. They decided to leave Adam Wilson where he lay. He had been stiff and sore on this morning, enough to hamper his movements. The vice-president's brother had the look of a man who has had enough.

'I'll raise some volunteers,' bellowed James

Tittle. The big man had apparently followed them forward to investigate. 'I said once I'd get this train to Denver if I had to carry it, and I meant it. I'll get some help.'

That boast was difficult to back up. Giles, the brakeman, worked for the railroad and therefore could hardly decline. A craggy-faced Minnesotan named Grange volunteered, saying, 'Back in Duluth this is good planting weather. I wonder where you Western folks got the reputation for being so hardy.'

Outside of these there were no offers to help, even though the passengers must have understood what would happen if they could not get the train rolling again – a night stranded on the frozen mountain slope.

They began removing sand from the locked boxes underneath the caboose and, shouldering a hundred-pound bag, easing their way forward to sand the rails in front of the halted locomotive.

Tom Pelt, shoveling out the hot ashes from the firebox, reported that he had no more than a few buckets left. The crew continued to haul sand – sometimes when men passed it was a near thing with the canyon dark and treacherous beside them, but it went well enough. The wind had become a gusting force, and men staggered under their burdens. The snow fell in heavy curtains still, but from time to time a hole would appear in the clouds and a shaft of light, blinding in its contrast, would strike their eyes.

All of the men worked with steady determination. Tom Pelt was a wonder. The Minnesotan, Grange, worked as if immune to the weather. James Tittle worked steadily, earning Tango's grudging admiration.

'What do you say, Danny?' Ned shouted up at the cab as the last half-dozen bags of sand were opened and spread along the rails – they were now a hundred feet or so ahead of the stranded locomotive.

Danny looked down worriedly. 'We've still got a full head of steam. If the drive wheels can find purchase, we should be all right.' He added uneasily, 'I don't know what else can be done.' Ned let the last of the workers string past him toward the passenger cars, thanking each in turn for his help, then he said to Danny: 'Let's get her rolling, Dan!'

Danny waited for big Tom Pelt to swing aboard, then he released the brake and applied the throttle. There was some hesitation. The train shuddered; the four massive drive wheels spun, clawing for purchase, sand and embers flew off the tracks. The locomotive seemed to barely inch forward. Then the big wheels caught traction and the train was rolling. Ned had remained beside the locomotive, watching fearfully, but now he could sense the motion building and he leaped on to the front platform of the next passenger car, entered the compartment and sagged on to a seat, tugging off his gloves, throwing his hat aside on the bench.

He watched the elated faces of the passengers, and scowled at the men who would do nothing to save themselves.

'Scoot over,' Marina said, nudging him.

Ned smiled wearily and made room for her. Studying him, she asked, 'Want to lie down in my room?'

'No. Tango's already getting suspicious of my attentions.'

'As well he should be,' Lady Marina Simpson said, taking Ned's arm as she snuggled up against his shoulder.

The train rumbled on. The grade seemed to flatten out a little. There would have been a beautiful view of the high Rockies beyond the windows on a sunny day. Now it remained closed to them by the gloomy curtain of low clouds and tangled snow.

Ned slept. It was close to midnight when he felt the train begin to slow again and he jerked awake, wondering what could have happened now – bandits, slipped rails, ice, rockslides, but Marina, still clinging to his arm, told him sleepily:

'It's Denver. I looked out a while ago. We're on flat ground. I could see hundreds of lights ahead.'

'Is it Denver?' Adam Wilson asked Tango who sat opposite him at the rear of the coach. The round man rose to peer out the window. 'By, God, it must be! You know, Tango, if there's another way to get back East, I'm taking it.'

'There's ways,' Tango said, lazily stretching his arms, 'but you wouldn't like them either.'

'No matter, I suppose,' Wilson replied. 'I'm going to enjoy this for now. Enjoy the luxury of one of the only cities in this god-forsaken West of yours.'

'Don't relax yet,' Tango told him. Wilson looked at the hatless, sleepy-eyed man with puzzlement.

'I don't get you, Tango.'

'It's like this: I have a feeling that a part of this was an attempt to stop you from reaching Denver. Not all of it, of course, but—'

'But you said those men came to hijack the train!'

'They did, yes. But after thinking it over, I think they also wanted you to perish out on the plains.'

'All of the other passengers. . . .' Wilson said in astonishment.

130

'Whoever's behind this was unconcerned with their life or death. Besides, with all of the passengers out there, you were just one of a bunch of travelers caught in the tragedy.'

'But you can't be sure!'

'No, sir. I'm seldom sure of anything, but I think you ought to take precautions before you meet with the territorial governor or whoever it is that you've come here to hold your talks with. If someone did try to cast you from the train into a winter storm, unconcerned about how many other deaths it might cause – well, that sort of man is not likely to just give up now.'

'But, Tango . . .' Wilson's brow was furrowed, his face pale. Tango was sorry that he had stepped on the little man's happiness, but he felt he should speak up. 'I'll be careful,' was all a now-deflated Wilson could say.

Ned met Tango half an hour on, just as the train began braking for the station, the lights of the incredibly large city of Denver blinking around them beneath the dissipating storm clouds. 'What now?' Ned asked. 'We're going to have to file a report – a long report with the railroad.'

'I don't think it's a good idea to roust them from their beds, do you, Ned? Let's let them get their rest and try to catch some sleep ourselves.'

'I have to disagree with you, my friend – much as I could use some rest, I think we should rouse the board members. If they haven't paid the ransom for the train yet, they need to know that it's been recovered. They won't be asleep anyway, or at least not sleeping well – with this on their minds.'

Tango sighed. Looking pained, he nodded his agreement. 'All right then, where do we start?'

'Charlie Boggs will be at the depot, minding the telegraph. We can have him round up a few men and send them to the houses of the board members. They live in the same general area, north of town. What do they call that section?'

'I wouldn't know,' Tango said drily. 'No one's ever invited me to one of their lawn parties out there.'

'Forget it. I'll see about notifying the board members. You can ask at the Golden Hotel if we can use their conference room for the meeting. We can all find accommodations there. When I'm through talking to Charlie, I'll return to the train, and find Marina. See if you can round up Wilson and escort him to the hotel – seeing as you're the one who's managed to make a nervous wreck of him.'

'All right,' Tango agreed unhappily. 'I just need

to get my traveling bag. I travel light. You go talk to Boggs. You know, Ned, you are going to make a lot of people unhappy one way or the other on this night.'

'Don't I know it?' Ned Chambers said with a tilted grin.

Within fifteen minutes Tango was escorting an uneasy Adam Wilson along Denver's dark streets toward the Golden Hotel. Wilson, who had left his baggage for the railroad to deliver later, had his hands thrust deeply into his coat pockets against the chill of the night. His eyes darted this way and that, seeing imagined menace in every shadow or suddenly appearing man. Ned was right, Tango supposed; he should not have told Wilson that he was probably still in danger.

The brightness of the vast interior of the hotel lobby revived Wilson's spirits. The gaslight glow showed a still concerned face which had regained some of its ruddy color. Tango, who was well known to the hotel personnel, found a room for himself, one for Wilson and two more, side by side, for Ned and Marina. Tango took the best rooms they had – it didn't trouble him: the railroad was going to pay for them.

With Tango it was a regular thing. Every week or so, after days spent sleeping cramped on a train seat, he allowed himself the luxury of stretching out on a real bed in a decent hotel. No one from the Colorado & Eastern had ever objected to his routine.

By the time Tango had gotten Wilson settled and tugged off his boots, Ned had arrived. The door to Tango's gold-and-cream-colored room was open. Ned came in, glancing around at the crystal lamps and the heavy mulberry carpet. 'I don't know how you get away with it,' Ned commented.

'They know my worth,' Tango said with a smile. He was ready to stretch out on a double-wide bed with a carved gilt headboard and a plum-colored coverlet.

'You might as well put your boots back on and brush off,' Ned said. 'Messengers have been sent to the homes of the board members. They'll be arriving within the hour.'

'What about my bath?' Tango complained, looking at his trail-stained clothes with the smears of coal dust clinging to them.

'Later. Change your shirt and let's get going.'

'You're a hard man, Ned,' Tango grumbled, but he reached for his travel bag and made his way to the bathroom – one of the remarkable new innovations at the Golden Hotel which Tango much appreciated.

He emerged a few minutes later wearing a deep-blue shirt, still creased from being folded in his bag, grabbed his hat, without which he did not feel dressed, and nodded to Ned. They went down the half-circular staircase and crossed the thick maroon carpet to the conference room to face the sleepy-eyed board members, none of whom wore a pleasant expression.

The board president, Emerson Cox half-rose from his chair and bellowed at the two as they entered.

'Where's my damned train, you incompetent bastards!'

NINE

Tango was the nearest to the red-faced, balding president of the board of directors, and he flushed and started to answer. Ned touched Tango's elbow, knowing that Tango was ready to fire back angrily, possibly losing his job and Ned's own in the process. Tango glanced at Ned Chambers, clamped his jaw shut and turned one of the high-backed chairs from the table to sit on.

'We brought the train through,' Ned said without embellishment. Emerson Cox goggled at him as did the other two men there – Clayton Ford with his slicked-down hair and waxed mustache and Eustace Plunkett with his strange, expressionless blue eyes peering through round, thick-lensed spectacles.

'What do you mean!' Cox continued in his bellowing tone.

'Just what I said – we brought the train through.'

'Want me to walk you over to the station?' Tango said before another sharp glance from Ned caused him to fall silent again.

'But how. . . ?' Cox half rose from behind the long mahogany table. 'We understood it was missing – stolen. When the train did not arrive on time, we were obliged to pay a huge sum to recover it.'

'Should have had a little more faith in your hired incompetent bastards,' Tango muttered.

'I wish you could have recovered the train and delivered it before we paid the ransom,' Clayton Ford muttered.

'We did the best we could under the circumstances,' Ned said apologetically.

'What were the circumstances exactly?' Eustace Plunkett asked, leaning forward across the table, hands clasped, his bright little blue eyes probing.

'There's really not the time to go into all of that right now,' Ned said. 'Tomorrow I'll begin writing a complete report on the events.'

Plunkett, looking as if he had been snubbed, leaned back, hands flat on the table, his expressionless eyes still fixed on Ned's face.

Clayton Ford asked anxiously, 'What about the vice-president's brother? Is he all right?'

'Adam Wilson is upstairs in this hotel at the moment,' Ned Chambers said. 'Hopefully he's resting well.'

'That was a rough welcome to Colorado for him,' Ford continued. 'As you know, Ned, the gold interests are trying to keep Colorado out of the Union. They feel the government merely wants control of their mines and of the wealth produced here. The railroad, on the other hand, wants to open the Territory up to commerce. It would mean much more in the way of contracts, many more family settlers arriving, small businesses. I know the way these gold strikes are – boom times and bust. Denver itself could become a ghost town if we are to continue to place reliance on the gold and silver strikes only. . . .'

'What has all of this got to do with the stolen train, Clayton?' Plunkett asked wearily.

'It's just that if we could prove that the big mine operators were behind it. . . .'

'They weren't!' Drew Tango snapped angrily, sitting up in his chair. 'Oh, they may have supplied a few tough men, some of their so-called 'regulators' to do the rough work, but the mining interests weren't behind the scheme.'

'You must be mistaken, Mr Tango,' Emerson Cox said, his eyes growing dark with censure.

He, it seemed, had already made up his mind who was responsible. 'Who would you blame if not the big mine operators? A random gang of outlaws? Indians?' This last he said sarcastically. Ned glanced at Tango, hoping his friend would not explode with his occasional fury. It could cost both of them their jobs. Instead, Tango answered in a cool, almost matter-of-fact voice.

'Where's Russell Blair? Is he or is he not a member of the board of directors? There are only the three of you here. Where is Blair?'

'I assume—' Cox began.

'You men do a lot of assuming,' interrupted Tango who sometimes did not seem to care whether he was employed or not, the way he challenged authority. 'When I was among the bandits in their camp – never mind how I got there; Ned, I'm sure, will include all of that in his report – I was told by the robbers that Russ Blair was behind the plan to capture the train.'

'That's reckless slander!' Plunkett said. 'An unsubstantiated, vile allegation.'

'So,' Tango asked softly, 'where, then, is Russ Blair? The ransom was paid and he's gone. Forgive my wild speculation, gentlemen – I only know what I heard and what I now see.'

There was a silence in the room. Then Emerson

Cox looked to Clayton Ford. 'Russell did receive the demand note. The money was paid to the robbers through Russell since he said he had contacts with them. I don't like the thought, but . . . Plunkett, get a man out to Russell Blair's house right now. Tell him we need to see him immediately.'

'You'll not find him there,' Tango said, rising. 'You might be able to run him down, since he won't be able to use the eastbound train to make his escape now, as was likely his original intention.'

'Russell did say something about going East to see his sister when this crisis was over,' Clayton Ford said thoughtfully, now not so certain of his friend's uninvolvement.

'I'm going to sleep,' Tango said. He turned and started toward the door. 'Any more questions will have to wait until morning.'

Although each of the board members thought privately that Drew Tango was an arrogant, tiresome man, no one said a word to stop him. They exchanged glances, realizing that they had run out of questions. Without words passing between them they rose, feeling the need for sleep themselves on this night.

Ned Chambers watched them go one by one, rose heavily from his own chair and started upstairs. He, too, needed some rest, and he meant to take care of that but he wished to, needed to, talk to Marina Simpson if only for a few minutes before he slept. That completed, he would not have to worry about his dreams on this night. They would be warm, gentle and comforting.

The sun was a low, red glowing ball in the east, coloring the new snow when Ned looked out of his window, stretched and went downstairs to meet Tango in the coffee room adjoining the elegant lobby of the Golden Hotel. He found Tango hovering over a cup of coffee, several breakfast plates stacked and pushed to one side of the table.

'Sleep well?' Tango asked as Ned seated himself and raised a finger in the direction of a harried-looking waitress.

'Hardly.' Ned reached into the inside pocket of his coat and removed a stack of folded yellow papers.

'That the report?'

'It is. Do you know how hard it was to reduce all that we went through to a few thousand words?'

'No, and I don't want to know. That's why they pay you the big money,' Tango said with a grin, knowing that Ned Chambers made only twenty dollars a month more than he himself did.

141

'Yes,' Ned said sourly as the waitress poured him a cup of coffee. 'There's another meeting of the board this morning – you'll come, won't you?'

'What do they need me for?' Tango asked reasonably. 'Anything I could tell them you've already written down.'

'All right, then,' Ned said with some disgust. He changed the subject. 'I've seen Frank Polk – he's doing much better – and he's agreed to tell them what he knows.'

'Good for him,' Tango said, stretching his arms over his head.

'You're acting like this is over, Tango.'

'It is as far as I'm concerned. I'm only a line-rider. You on the other hand are a railroad detective. I don't investigate; I only ride the rails.'

'Don't you have a personal interest in all of this?'

'Not that personal,' Tango said, reaching for his hat which rested on the chair beside him. 'What do you want me to do? Try to ride down Russell Blair – assuming we could know which way he's gone?'

'We could try,' Ned said insistently.

'Nope,' Tango replied, rising. 'I only use two forms of transportation – the railroad and my feet. I don't cotton to horses.'

'I remember a few years ago that you actually quit the job to ride after some outlaws.'

'That,' Tango said, '*was* personal. This isn't.'

'You're a hard man, Drew Tango,' Ned said.

'Am I not? Go on and turn in your report. Me, I'm taking a bath and maybe a daytime nap. The eastbound train doesn't pull out until early evening.'

'All right,' Ned grumbled, 'if that's the way it is.'

'That's the way it is, Ned. You go try to find Russ Blair if that's what you want to do. Me, I'm riding the rails East.'

Tango had it in mind to clean his guns, visit the closest saloon, buy some new clothes and, as he had told Ned, try taking another nap before the long ride on the eastbound train which had already been long delayed due to the trouble down the line. Heading up the curved staircase to the upper floor of the Golden he met Marina coming down, a hatbox in her hands. 'Good morning, Princess,' Tango said lightly.

'Have you seen Ned, Tango?'

'Yes. He was just going to eat breakfast. Then he has that meeting with the railroad board.'

'I know. He was up working on that report until all hours. I could see the light under the connecting door. He so wants to do things right.'

143

'That's Ned,' Tango commented.

'You – you're not like him at all, are you?'

'No. I suppose we're different pups whelped out of the same bitch.'

'Ah,' Marina said with a shaky smile, 'the reason I'm glad I am an American – in Nottingham someone would slap you for speaking that way.' Tango only looked puzzled. 'I need your help, Tango, if you have a little while.'

'I suppose I have a little time. What is it you need?'

'I have to go over to Berkshire's, if you know what that is.'

'I have no idea.'

'Well, it's a jewelry store. I mean to sell some of my gewgaws. I can't see the time coming when I will wish to wear a diamond tiara out here.'

'If it's cash money you need . . .' Tango said, beginning an offer.

'No, Tango.' She touched his wrist. 'I thank you, but I believe – hope – I can raise a quarter of a million dollars on what I'm carrying with me.' She hoisted the hatbox. 'I'd just like you to accompany me for protection, if you would. I'd ask Ned, of course, but he's so busy right now.'

How much Marina actually raised Tango did not know, and did not ask, but after going through a session with the man in charge of appraisals at Berkshire's Jewelry Store and a visit to the bank to open an account, it was obvious that her spirits were lighter.

'How are the steaks at the restaurant?' she asked Tango on the way back to the hotel.

'Haven't tried one yet.'

'Let's do it now, shall we? I'm buying,' Marina said.

'I had a big breakfast, but my stomach wouldn't mind.'

They each had a steak and baked potato, corn on the cob and apple pie for lunch, speaking only of trivialities. When they were finished, napkins folded, Tango said: 'If you won't be needing me anymore. . . .'

'No, thank you, Tango. I am just going to find a real estate office and do some preliminary searches.'

'You mean to stay around Denver then?'

'Yes, we . . . I thought it might be best to rent a house over the winter, and then when spring arrives, to look for a place outside of town.'

'Sounds like a good idea. By then you'll know if you want to stay in the city or go upcountry.' With a dog, a little kitten and a baby cradle, Tango thought – angry for some reason. He studied the dark, well-groomed Lady Simpson, saw deep hap-

145

piness in her eyes, and half-cursed Ned Chambers for his amazing luck. 'I've got to be going now,' he said, rising abruptly.

So Ned and Marina were going to be settling down – and Tango would keep on riding the rails. Probably forever. So what! It was a good life.

He scuffed his way across the lobby and out the front door, to watch the high riding sun glint off the snow-clad purple mountain peaks. Then Tango started for the dry-goods store across the street. He needed some new duds, and he decided right then that he would also purchase the finest Stetson in the store. He owed himself that much. And he had pocket money; the way he lived, he spent nothing for food, nor for accommodations. His pay wasn't that bad, either. His spirits lifted as he crossed the slush-covered street. It was a good life – let Ned and Marina try it their way. Tango knew deep inside that he would get antsy locked down in a house, seeing the same town every day. He needed to ride the rails. Why, he could not have said, but he always felt as if he were gaining ground, going somewhere even if the next day brought him back to where he had started from.

He had just reached the plankwalk opposite when Ned Chambers, breathless, hatless, caught up with him.

'Tango – Russell Blair is going to ride the east-bound train today!'

'How do you know?'

'Charlie Boggs sold him a ticket. He thought it was important, so he came over to the railroad office to report it. The board of directors had posted a reward for any information. Blair must be hanging around the depot waiting for the 5.05. The way his mind works, that would be the only means of escape he could think of.'

'Talk to the yard police,' Tango advised. 'That's their job.'

'Tango, help me finish this up,' Ned pleaded. 'The yard cops are mostly pensioners; hardly a one of them has a tooth left in his head. They are good at running off hobos and chasing stray dogs away, but Blair has all that money, and a purpose. Charlie Boggs said that there were two rough men with Blair. Probably mine regulators, hired guns, judging by Blair's past preference for those types.

'What do you want?' Tango said after an extended silence.

'I want you to help me root him out,' Ned said. 'Who else would I want beside me in a gunfight?'

'I was just going to buy a new hat,' Tango said inconsequentially. 'But – come on, Ned, let's go see if we can get ourselves killed!'

147

The railroad yard was relatively deserted on this chill afternoon. Luggage was being loaded, and freight for the east. The railroad crew stood in bunches, talking. Others filled the boiler of the locomotive, loaded wood on to the tender and performed a hundred other routine tasks in preparation for departure.

It was too early for the passengers to begin appearing. On the bench behind the station, two elderly men whittled and exchanged old, old jokes. A dog with one folded ear watched them with apparent amusement, his pink tongue lolling.

They spotted Charlie Boggs, the cadaverous station-master and went his way.

'Any sign of Blair yet?' Ned Chambers asked.

'No, but I'm keeping a sharp eye out for him.'

'He didn't board the train early?' Tango inquired.

'No, sir,' Boggs replied, apparently miffed by the question. 'I had my eye on it all the time. Besides,' he added, 'the clean-up crew is still on board sweeping out the aisles, touching up the scuffs on the seats and all. He's not on board.'

'Well,' Tango said, his eyes searching the network of rails. 'I guess we'd better get busy and find him. He sure wouldn't risk wandering around town. He has to be near by.'

They walked the length of the train headed by engine number 12, both feeling tense. Blair was around, had to be. Passing the locomotive they spotted a familiar face. Tom Pelt, grinning widely, leaned out and waved his arm at them.

'Got a job, I see,' Tango said.

'Thanks to you, Mr Tango – and to Danny Short. Even the vice-president's brother recommended me to the railroad. You can't get a better endorsement than that.'

'I guess not. I'm just happy that it's working out for you.'

'What's happening in the board room?' Ned wanted to know.

'Nothing much – they asked Danny what had happened back there, and then Frank Polk. Danny asked about getting his own train, but they said he hadn't had enough experience yet.'

'He'll make it – with Frank's help.'

'Sure he will. Both he and Mr Polk have been put on leave while they recuperate, although Danny said he didn't need no rest.'

'We wanted to ask you about a man . . .' Ned Chambers said.

'You mean this Russell Blair? Mr Boggs told us

all to keep alert for him.' Tom Pelt shook his head. 'If he's the one who just stranded all those people out there in the middle of a blizzard, I'd like to get my hands on him myself.'

Tango pitied any man that the massive kid ever got his hands on – except for Russell Blair.

Tango and Ned trudged on. 'He's got to be here somewhere,' Ned was convinced.

'There are a lot of places to hole up,' Tango said, surveying the crowded station with its waiting locomotives, freight cars and swarms of outbuildings.

'True, but we know where he wants to go – to engine number 12, and we know what time. He has to be there before 5.05.'

'That does give us an advantage,' Tango said, 'but don't forget he is supposed to have two hired guns with him. And they'll fight – if not for Blair, for the money he's carrying.'

'I know, but all we can do is wait for them to come to us, Tango. We can't search the entire yard.'

'We can enlist the yard police. Maybe they wouldn't be much use in a gunfight, but they can raise a holler if they spot those three. I don't know the man, Ned; what's your memory of his looks?'

'He's a bulky man, maybe slovenly is a better

word. You know, carrying a lot of desk-fat. When I saw him last he wore a wide-flourishing red mustache.'

'Well, he could have shaved the mustache off and grown a few whiskers,' Tango said thoughtfully, 'but he won't be able to disguise his weight. Let's have a meeting with the yard cops.'

That done, there was nothing left for Tango and Ned to do but to wait as the final preparation of the train was completed. The arrival of eastbound passengers at the station flowed slowly past them as departure time neared. Number 12 already had a head of steam as the lonesome sun began to lower itself toward the mountains where it glinted, exploded with deep color and golden slashes across the skies, and faded.

'What time is it?' Tango asked as he glanced back along the train to watch a porter assist a pretty young woman on to the train.

'Almost five o'clock,' Ned said, glancing at his steel watch.

'Well, he's got to come soon – if he's coming at all.'

'He'll come,' Ned was certain. 'The man I know isn't likely to fork a bronc and head for the far country. He likes his comfort too much.'

'Who's that?' Tango asked, nudging Ned.

'Never seen him before, have you?' They were both watching a man with a long-fringed buckskin coat who seemed to be wandering aimlessly across the sundown-stained train yard.

'Somebody looking for a free ride?' Ned suggested.

'I think he's scouting the situation out,' Tango said, looking again at the hefty, beetle-browed stranger. 'Follow my lead, but keep your eye on him.'

Then Tango crouched down, spread his arms wide, rose and elevated his pointing finger to indicate the smokestack of Number 12. As Ned kept one eye on the stranger, Tango shook his head angrily. Then he got to the ground and slithered forward until his head was nearly under the cow-catcher.

'What in hell are you supposed to be?' Ned Chambers asked.

'I'm a railroad inspector,' Tango hissed back.

'Doing. . . ?'

'Doing what ever railroad inspectors do. How should I know! Where's our man?'

'Wandering back toward the fuel barn,' Ned said, crouching down to look at whatever imaginary defect Tango was supposed to have found.

'He's out of sight now. Can we stop the charade?'

Tango wriggled out again. 'I didn't want whoever it was to see two armed men just standing here observing,' Tango said, dusting off his clothes. 'I think that was our man – one of them. Let's move toward the rear of the train.'

'Hold it,' Ned said, gripping Tango's arm. 'Your instincts were right – here they come.'

Tango glanced briefly that way, seeing two rough-looking men flanking a shambling, heavy-set man with a stubble of reddish beard. Tango continued to give his impersonation of an inspector dressing down a negligent employee.

'Is that him?' Tango asked.

'It has to be,' Ned answered, peering into the dusky shadows. He looked briefly at his watch. 'It's five o'clock straight up.'

'All right – do you want to wait for them or walk out and face them?'

'I don't want lead flying around the passengers,' Ned said, glancing to where a half-dozen more people were boarding the train in the purple twilight.

'No, you're right. Let's take a stroll toward the depot. I'll gesture a lot, make it look like I'm still upset about something. We'll angle slowly toward them. Ned – watch it – they'll be primed to shoot.'

153

'If only Blair hasn't recognized me, though that seems unlikely in this light.'

'Keep your hat tugged low and your hand near your Colt,' Tango advised in a near-whisper, then he began gesticulating again, moving his lips soundlessly. The pantomime worked until they were within fifty feet of the three approaching men. Then all hell broke loose.

TEN

Tango and Ned saw Blair halt abruptly, saw him goggle and point at them. They could clearly hear him say, 'Chambers,' then his bodyguards began shooting. A pair of shots rang out and two bullets whipped past Ned and Tango to bore into the station-house wall. Tango threw himself to the ground which was rough gravel between the various sets of rails, but Ned ill-advisedly assumed a dueler's stance and fired back from an erect position. His first shot missed, whining off something made of solid metal, but his second bullet found flesh, and as Tango watched one of the regulators dropped his pistol and grabbed the calf of his leg, hopping away across the rail yard, unwilling to play the game out.

The second gunhand was made of sterner stuff.

He drew and faced down Ned with no hesitation showing in his dark, beetle-browed face. He fired deliberately, twice, and both bullets seemed to tag Ned. One of them seemed inconsequential, plucking at the shoulder of his suit coat, but the second one hit flesh and bone. Tango saw Ned double over, saw him fire a round into the gravel at his feet.

In the near-darkness, Tango lifted himself to one knee and fired his own weapon. Not once, but four times. The spinning .44 slugs caught the bodyguard and he went into a twisted, tortuous dance before he flung his arms skyward and flopped to the hard earth.

Russell Blair took off at a dead run. Or as close to one as the grossly obese man could manage. Despair propelled the big man along. He seemed to be heading back to the great wood barn where the three men had been hiding. He looked across his shoulder, saw the younger, fitter Tango pursuing him and tried to fire across his shoulder with his pistol. The shot was miles wide, and Tango continued grimly on.

Blair was panting loudly enough for Tango to hear. He plunged on through the gathering shadows, a helpless quarry. There was no spring in his legs, and he could barely lift his feet. His boot toe stubbed itself on the rail of one of the shunting tracks and the big man flopped and rolled inelegantly down, skinning his face, hands and knees. With a sick moan he tried to rise to his feet, but it was no good.

Tango planted his boot in the middle of Blair's back and shoved him down hard.

'That's it, Blair,' Tango said, his gun pointed at the back of Russell Blair's neck. 'Come along with me now and I'll find you a nice quiet place to rest up.'

Ned was trying to rise as Tango prodded Blair back toward him. 'Just sit there, Ned. I'll get you some help.'

Without answering, Ned nodded, crossed his legs and sat with his hair hanging in his eyes. From the depot building Tango saw Charlie Boggs appear, flanked by a pair of armed railroad guards.

Number 12's whistle blew; its bell rang four times. The 5.05 was right on schedule.

The next day Drew Tango took his accustomed seat on the eastbound morning train. The gunhand who had run off had been captured at a doctor's office. The money Russell Blair had extorted from the railroad had been found. Ned Chambers was in the hotel with a tender nurse to watch over him. Adam Wilson was meeting with the territorial governor, talking about whatever politicians talk about when they're out of the public eye. Frank Polk was mending. . . .

The train jerked and started on its way, the wheels settling into a familiar, rhythmical pattern, drawing away from the railroad yard, away from Denver. It was like leaving all civilization behind, a sensation Tango had always liked. The locomotive steamed along the track across the wide plateau and life became a little simpler.

'Excuse me?'

Tango looked up to see a young woman with hair so blond as to approach white. Her eyes were cornflower blue. She was slender, had a pert nose and a mouth which was full. Her expression was questioning. She had on a blue gingham dress and a wide straw hat with a blue ribbon tie.

'Yes?'

'I'm sorry,' she said, speaking in little puffs of breath. 'The coach is rather full. I was wondering if . . . if you wouldn't mind if I sat here.'

Mind? Tango rose and stepped into the aisle so the girl could take the window seat. There was a confident yet bashful manner about her. She smiled brightly as she settled into the seat. Tango could smell her clean scent like dew in the morning, a warm garden scent he could not identify.

'Going home?' he asked.

'Only for a visit. Denver's my home now,' she said, looking out at the long sunlit plains, the high peaks beyond. 'It's a grand land, isn't it?'

'Some find it melancholy with civilized places so far apart.'

'Oh, I know. I'd feel the same way I suppose, if I were new out here, but I've found a place where I feel I belong. What is it you do, Mister. . . ?'

'Drew Tango,' he supplied. 'What do I do?' Tango laughed faintly. 'I ride the rails, miss.'

'Ride the rails? You mean you just go back and forth and forth and back?'

'That's about it, I suppose,' Tango had to admit.

'Well, that would . . .' the girl smiled and faltered. 'That seems to me as if it might get a little boring after a while, although I suppose it must have its moments of excitement.'

A voice thundered through the railroad car.

'Put all of your valuables in the bag! I mean it, lady!'

Tango glanced up to see a familiar face. It was Mickey Dent, the small-time hoodlum and former member of the Chris Stilton gang. Tango had last seen him at the way station where they had taken shelter after leaving the captured train. Dent had his hair slicked back, parted in the middle, dressed down with pomade, but he couldn't do anything to

159

disguise those crossed front teeth of his. He was brandishing a pistol and carrying a bag. He moved slowly down the aisle toward Tango's seat. A train porter watched him from behind as Mickey Dent bullied his way along.

'Give me that watch, mister, or I'll blow your head off. Lady, don't be trying to hide that ring! Give it up. Now! Hurry up!'

Tango uncoiled himself from the seat and stood in front of the would-be train robber. Mickey Dent gawked at Tango, recognizing him.

'You still haven't learned to ask for things nicely, have you, Mickey?'

Dent didn't hesitate to shoot, but his skill was no match for Tango's. The robber shot through the ceiling of the coach as Tango's bullet struck his heart. Waving his arms frantically, throwing his scavenged loot into the air, Dent staggered back and died in the aisle.

Tango holstered his pistol and said to the astonished porter, 'Lou, place this man in the baggage car, will you?'

Tango wiped a hand across his hair and returned to his seat where the young woman watched him with incredulous eyes.

'Now then,' Drew Tango asked her, 'what were we talking about?'